Sojourn
A Woman In Exile

I0652974

RASHI SHRIVASTAVA

Sojourn

This is a work of fiction. Names, characters, businesses, places, events and incidents are either the products of the author's imagination or used in a fictitious manner. Any resemblance to actual persons, living or dead, or actual events is purely coincidental.

First published in August 2017 by
Becomeshakespeare.com
Wordit Content Design & Editing Services Pvt Ltd
Unit - 26, Building A-1, Nr Wadala RTO, Wadala (East),
Mumbai 400037, India
T: +91 8080226699

©

ISBN: 978-93-86487-42-1

It was as if her soul was willing to bare itself to his love, like a tree whose leaves are shed at the mere sight of autumn.

Dedicated to stories that survived in spite of Love.

ACKNOWLEDGMENTS

There are people without whom I could not have had the encouragement to proceed with this Sisyphean task of writing endlessly, without fruition.

My parents, especially my mother who didn't really know about this book, until she read the first draft. Thank you for those cathartic tears which made me believe in myself and in the effect of my story.

Peter J. Benny, author of *Deja Moo* (published on Amazon Kindle) for being the first beta reader of the nubile draft of this book and for suggesting genuine changes and also opening my mind to accept those changes.

Katie Wheeler, founder of Blueberry Books, my editor. Without you, this narrative would have been raw. You were patient enough to delete out versions of Indian English from the book and enhance the clarity. Also, I owe 'Veer' to you.

Twitter. Co. for making such a platform where I could meet these two and other such wonderful people, from across the globe.

Dr. Pramesh Ratnakar, author of the *Centurion – The Father, The Son and the Spirit Of Cricket* (published by Harper Collins India) and my former professor, for all the publishing advice and for writing out a tailor made foreword to this book.

Mrs. Jayashree Guha, my English teacher from school, to whom I extend my most heartfelt gratitude because she made me believe in the literary capacity I possessed.

My PR Agency, Mad Pro Media and my manager, Nikhita Anil for shouldering the responsibility of getting this book released.

Most importantly, I would like to thank each of the authors I have read, living or dead, who was the major inspiration behind me being able to write.

Thank you ☺

PREFACE

It is hard to put words together as I attempt to draft out a 'Preface' for my first book. It's as if I'm living a dream that was hard to fulfil and is still harder to realise as fulfilled.

To begin with, "Sojourn – A Woman in Exile" was not meant to be as how it stands at present, all dressed up in a book cover, contents and polished pages. It was a seed, conceived a year ago in February 2016. The last scene of the novel was what came first to my mind, and I allowed myself to go with the flow. It was not just my hand, working constantly on paper, but also my eyes, overflowing with tears as I put my heart onto the pages of that blue diary, which stands as a witness to the hours I spent scratching words on its dry pages with blue ink.

It is hard to believe, because not once did I stop and think about what I was writing or why I wrote it. It's hard to believe because I hadn't ever really put together fiction. I had done poetry and articles before, but something that had to be held together by a single thread of thought, was hard for me to imagine and compile as a book.

"Sojourn" is a story with a very simple and tragic plot, and an open end. However, what is endearing is the life and nature of its characters, whom I have tried to weave with utmost care and love. The protagonist Mira, is the one closest to my being because she is, somewhat an extension of myself, or rather what I believe myself to be. Veer, initially a nameless character, is a sketch of my imagination with inputs from people around me, who I observe every day. As they say, there are a million stories around us, we just need to read the right one and sit back and enjoy, as the characters come alive on paper.

This is not a story of right or wrong. I have left this heavy debate to be dealt with the readers. It's their story and they shall decide how they want to end the story of Mira and Veer, because each one of us has their own version of truth and morality. Not always, is the obvious morally right, the right thing for us.

On a concluding note, I extend my heartfelt gratitude to YOU, the reader, because it was your love for reading which made you buy this book and help me a bit, a small bit, in the process. I sincerely hope that you enjoy reading this book, as much as I enjoyed writing it.

Rashi Shrivastava
New Delhi, March 2017

FOREWORD

When one of your students, who was just the other day running around seeking admission in college, and who has not yet finished her Masters, rings you up and asks you whether you would write a foreword for her recently completed novel, you end up feeling, not 'elated' or 'honoured', but actually, rather worried. What if one were to read the novel and not like it? What if it turns out to be badly conceived, badly written, and a mawkish piece of writing?

In the case of young Rashi Shrivastava's first novel, these fears have proved to be wholly unfounded. She has produced an accomplished piece of writing, and I have no hesitation in declaring to whoever it may concern that not only did I enjoy reading through her novel, but felt both elated and honoured at being asked to write this foreword.

The narrative begins and ends with Mira, a thirty six year old single woman in Sikkim, working as an English professor at the local university. A dream opens the floodgates of her memories and emotions. She is reminded of Veer when she goes out for her morning jog, she is reminded of him while taking a bath, she is reminded of him by every gush of air that touches her face. Unable to carry on, she sits down at her favourite place set in the heart of a small district in Sikkim – Pelling. Her thoughts and yearnings overlap with the air of the mountains and the crisp, biting snow, and the tingling warmth of the mountain sun.

As Mira brings all to mind, we get to see that her cage of memories harbours childhood pains, a distorted parent child relationship and an overarching love relationship that seemed destined for an idyllic togetherness, but actually ends up leading Mira to world of empty and lonely memories. The author uses a crisp third person narrative, along with the stream of consciousness technique, to dive into the mind of her protagonist.

At the end of the novel, Mira returns to the present and there is a symbolic turning over of a new leaf, or perhaps a new life. But then suddenly she is confronted with a surprise waiting on her doorstep - with an attendant moral dilemma. She has to make a choice, and the choice she makes would determine the course of her future life. But what is that choice – that is left for the reader to decide, based upon his or her personal understanding of love, relationships and moral rights or wrongs.

It is a solitary, meditative book that tolls you back to your sole self. The book seems to suggest that our sense of the "self", our sense of who we are, exists and evolves through the choices that we make as we seek coherence and continuity through the various

10

stages of our lives – the tragedies, the triumphs, celebrations and crises. At the end, Rashi Shrivastava's narrative leaves both Mira and us with an age-old question about 'true' love. Does it not necessarily involve the surrender of self? But then, what kind of life is one left with, once the self itself has been sacrificed?

The novel is short on story, short on characters and short on plot. But it has a lot of atmosphere, and – something not easy to achieve – an overarching mood that holds the all the elements of the narrative together. And then, there is Mira. She will most certainly visit you in your moments of solitude, and ask you difficult questions about the ardour of love, and about the sacrifices you made - or did not make - in the cause of love.

Pramesh Ratnakar
Associate Professor
Author of *Centurion: The Father, the Son and the Spirit of Cricket.*
(New Delhi: HarperCollins, 2012)

Sojourn

CONTENTS

Prologue

Eleven years had passed, and, still she stood where she had left him. The places had changed. The surroundings had changed. The people had changed. Age had changed her as well, but her eyes remained the same, hidden beneath the lightly smudged kohl. Only it seemed, that they had lost their light. That spark had been dimmed the day she left him behind.

Not much had changed in him, though. He stood in the hall wearing dark blue jeans and a crimson shirt, topped with a black jacket. Despite the numerous times she had taught him that collar upon collar was a fashion faux pas, he had made the same mistake that day. She wondered if he had done it deliberately, or perhaps, it was her imagination.

But there he was, after eleven years, standing in the square hall of her house, with his knees brushing against the adjacent sofa, the same height, build, face and smile, exactly as she remembered him.

Only his eyes seemed different to her, they weren't their sparkling usual. Maybe, it was the mist of her own eyes that she couldn't see deep or clearly enough. For a moment, her heart stopped pumping blood, rather it was pumping at such a furious speed that it benumbed her. After all, she had finally seen that face again after eleven years of pain and separation, eleven years of longing and yearning for his love, and his touch. She wanted to run to him, to

13

embrace him with her full strength, to amalgamate him into herself. But that had all been lost eleven years ago and this thought brought her back to reality.

His presence was paralysing, overwhelming and she was about to black out as she staggered on one foot, attempting to hold on to the adjacent sofa, when he came to the rescue.

"Mira," he said in a heavily choked voice and that was force enough to grip her, and to bring her back to her senses. Her name emanating from his lips had a healing effect on her, but she chose to remain silent.

SIKKIM

CHAPTER ONE

She was running in that old dilapidated house, turning as the house shaped itself on its own, taking form, maybe according to the directions she took. She looked left and right for some way, but instead she stepped into a hallway with a huge wooden door, a massive door, which seemed ancient to her. She found herself trying to push it open, getting restless when unable to do so. She felt a desperate rush to reach the other side, but the door just wouldn't budge. In a sudden turn of events, she found herself being pushed against the door and pulled through to the other side. She became aware of a sudden strange thumping against her chest. The moment that big door opened, she saw a strange figure – a greyish figure of a man standing, far away. Someone she didn't recognize but somewhere her heart knew that this was the figure of a man she had once known very well. The figure stepped out of the darkness, and she saw his face clearly, feeling a sudden burst of nostalgia and longing. She tried to reach out to him, to embrace him, but as she took her first step, the setting collapsed and the figure disappeared. She fell into a deep oblivion, a mass less pit, a space less darkness, and she tried to grab on to something for support but there was nothing around her. She was falling, still falling, deeper into chaos.

Mira woke up with a start. The dream. That dream again. It was the same dream, but today she was

17

trembling more than ever.

She felt as though she had a temperature as well. Her heart, which bore a sinking feeling, was beating loudly against her chest. Her breathing slowly subsided as she came to terms with reality observing the room around her. She had beads of sweat on her face and temples.

Mira had finally discovered the identity of the grey shadowy figure of a man who first appeared in this particular dream of hers seven years ago. She had known all along who this figure could be, but today she had seen his face. Of course it was him.

She raised her eyes to look at the window-sized picture of them hanging on the opposite wall. Yes, he was Veer. She was sure of reality now. The man in the dream was the man who had posed with her for a photograph in front of the Taj Mahal, all those years ago. That man had been and, somewhere still was the sole reason for her existence. The man she had loved, the man she had worshipped, and the man her heart still belonged to.

Koicha came bustling into the room. She was the woman who took care of Mira's house, and perhaps the only friend left to Mira. Koicha drew apart the curtains and started picking up the things that were lying about the room, mostly books, papers and clothes.

Mira watched her returning them to their rightful places. She always felt a sense of security with Koicha. There was no real reason for this feeling. Only that she felt it.

She had been working late, as she often did these

days, on her second novel. She was planning to write a historical romance and had been reading voraciously to find a suitable couple, from history, to indulge in. 'Antony and Cleopatra' appealed to her. They were passionate and driven by their sensuality, but a novel like that required extensive research, which resulted in late nights, books lying around and therefore an untidy room.

When Mira had first met Koicha or, rather, had first employed her, she had barely been able to read or write, except her own name in a very mechanical way. But Mira was patient, and had taught her not only to speak fluently in English, but also to read and write in the language. Little had she known that Koicha would be so quick to grasp the new knowledge and within a span of three years she would be able to read books by Enid Blyton and other children's fiction.

Teaching Koicha was not just a duty that Mira felt she must fulfil, rather, it was something that gave her extreme pleasure and a sense of satisfaction, feelings she had thought were lost to her. When Mira had first arrived in Sikkim, to settle here forever, she had never planned to make many contacts, let alone to get to know someone so personally. But somehow, from the very beginning, Koicha had been different. She was not only the first friend Mira had made in Sikkim, she was also the only friend she had made in eleven years.

Mira's life, here in Sikkim, was something completely different, almost the opposite of her previous life. The change had been deliberate and Mira had allowed only some strains of her previous life to taint her new existence and one of those extended threads was the collection of photographs that hung on the walls of her house, photographs of Veer. Some of them were pictures of them together and some of him alone. She glanced through them, as per her morning ritual, reminiscing for a moment in the memories that these photographs had captured.

Veer had not just been a part of Mira's life, he had been her life. That was why in moving away from him she had left behind, an entire part of her. The old Mira, who had been somewhat sociable, with a large group of friends always watching movies together or going out dancing, had all but vanished. Mira had secluded herself in that three bedroom wooden house, which she had rented in the Pelling district of North Sikkim. A house that she was soon going to buy once she received her second pay check from the publishers of her first novel.

Koicha was a short statured, north-eastern young woman, with eyes slightly narrowing at the edges and a freckled face complete with reddish pink cheeks. At two and thirty winters down, she was just four years younger than Mira. She had a habit of screwing up her nose whenever she was reflecting on something or was involved in deep thought. She was doing it now as she dusted the bookshelf in Mira's room. She opened her mouth to say something, but stopped short.

Mira, sitting cross legged on her bed and tying her hair up in a sturdy ponytail, noticed Koicha's indecision.

"Speak up, Koicha," she said, "what is bothering you?"

She was preparing herself to go for her morning walk, something she never missed. No matter how tired she was, she liked walking and running every day for about an hour, amidst the fog and beneath the clouds, on the roads of Pelling.

Inherently, she was much of a nature's person and believed that natural spaces and scenery could have a healing effect upon tampered souls. Mira herself had experienced this healing power of nature, at the time when she had needed it the most, which was after her separation from Veer.

"What should I make for breakfast?" Koicha said, eventually, "and what time is your class?"

Mira knew that this petite squinting nose had something else in mind because she could see Koicha debating within, whether to let out or not. Mira decided to give her some space and time to decide.

"Usual classes at 11.30. Just make me a cup of Bourn vita milk and an egg sandwich for today. And for lunch you can pack me two *chapattis* and make whatever vegetable you feel like, but not boiled potatoes again, please!" Mira replied.

Koicha smiled.

One thing that deserved a special mention was that Mira never treated Koicha as a housekeeper, but always as a friend. Something hard to find in Indian societies, but she was comfortable about it. Mira enjoyed sharing meals together and, at times, going out for walks and grocery shopping. Now that Koicha knew how to read, write and even speak fluently in English, Mira had often urged her to take her studies further and pursue some other career, but Koicha preferred to stay with Mira and continue learning under her guidance. Mira was glad, in some ways, that Koicha had never heeded her encouragement to study elsewhere. She derived a great sense of happiness in teaching Koicha, not solely because she wanted to educate her but, also, because it reminded her of the times she taught Veer, pointing out grammatical errors in his ill framed sentences. Though he was the son of an English teacher, he had always hated grammar and his writing had needed a lot of reworking to meet Mira's standards.

Koicha, too, would have hated leaving, whether for her studies or some other career. She wanted to be with Mira, her *'Didi'* till the time the man in the photographs came back to her friend. She usually referred to him as *'Saheb'*. She was so sure that it would happen someday and she was ready to sacrifice her future for that.

"How about fried cottage cheese and capsicum?" Koicha said.

"Perfect!" Mira said, beginning to stretch out her shoulders before her walk.

Koicha smiled to see her sitting in the middle of the, now tidy, room, with the man in the photograph watching over her.

CHAPTER TWO

Mira set out of her house, taking steep steps down the hill to reach the main road. Of course, there wasn't any real main road in the mountains. Her house was built on an elevation, a quiet hill with terraced steps that connected the house to the main road, which hardly ever had any vehicles treading on it. There were no other houses or shops in the vicinity and Mira had been entranced by this house when she had seen it a decade ago. It had been exactly what she had wanted – isolation and not many souls nearby, only the ones she permitted to be around her.

She took her usual route, although there weren't many options on the hill road. One could either go left or right. Mira took the left. Her wrist watch showed 7:30 in the morning, and Pelling was wide awake. She could see people moving about their houses or on the roads. There were some people who knew her, but not many, even though she had spent ten years in the neighbourhood. Before the publication of her first book, the number of people she knew was even less. After that, however, there were times when some of the faces recognized her from her book, the young people especially. Mira had become a local celebrity. Though she had not really wanted attention, she enjoyed seeing the spark of recognition in the eyes of the people around her.

Dressed in a black and yellow tracksuit with her hair tied back in a long ponytail, she began by taking long strides, alternating them with short intervals of sprinting. These long walks and runs amidst the trees played an important role in Mira's life. These spaces combined with the fresh morning breeze, cold, but rejuvenating, when hit her face, made her feel as though the cells of her body were replenishing themselves, the pores on her body opening up and healing her inside out.

Mira was at present, six and thirty winters down, nearing forty in a few years, but she seemed to have aged beautifully. Her beauty was not one at the expense of heavy cosmetics, unlike the need of every woman of her times. It was because of her active dalliance with nature, the long walks, and the abundance of fresh air around her. She believed that the greener it was around you, the merrier you were and the prettier you looked. Mira's healing process had been aided by all the naturalness around her.

It was not only after leaving Veer behind that she had developed this longing for nature, rather, she had always been this way. Though Mira had spent her childhood in New Delhi, definitely one of the most polluted cities of India, she had never really had a chance to fret about the pollution. Her neighbourhood had been an agricultural space, embellished with thousands of trees and greenery all around. Her favourite season had always been autumn. Veer had always found this preference of her peculiar, but he had also known that Mira had a deeper insight into some things. Where other people rejoiced in spring as the season of rejuvenation, Mira rejoiced in autumn, to see the leaves continuously being shed from the trees. She grew ecstatic in this shower of leaves. She loved the red and orange hues, and the delight she felt while walking beneath the canopy of trees with the soft breeze brushing against her body and the leaves, both big and small, falling all around her, some resting, entangled in her hair.

Mira had possessed long hair since childhood, though not very long. She had always wanted waist long hair while she was in Delhi. She found it amusing that while she was with him, she had never been able to achieve the kind of hair he loved. Veer had always entreated her not to cut her hair and to let it grow endlessly, because she had gorgeous hair and if some length could be added, it would be just perfect. Ironically, she had only been able to achieve that perfection when there was no one to appreciate it, no one except Koicha. Life can never stop throwing stones at you and one has to abide by all that life has to offer, even if it is just an irony and mockery.

This life, surrounded by nature, was what Mira had always imagined for herself, unconsciously of course. She never thought, even for a second, that it would eventually come true, and that Mira would really get to live this life, but by paying a huge price for it. By losing Veer to the world, she had gained her inner space. It was a lost bargain, but the only deal she could have had. Except, she had never really believed that she had lost him. He lived with her, through her and would continue to do so till the very last of her existence.

However, for a change and for a moment, Mira was not thinking directly about Veer. He had not ceased to be a part of her thought process in the past eleven years, and each morning, she was reminded of him by a peculiar scene in the woods.

25

There was an uncut hill at the top of a mountain, covered in green velvet and green woods and, amidst all that greenery, she could see a flock of colourful, extremely petite birds, almost like finches, trying to fly. She often stopped to watch them, especially the younger ones, because it seemed to her that these birds were not well adapted to flying. They were supposed to be birds of the woods. Mira had gathered from the locals that these birds had been flightless, but had learnt to fly, over time, over all these years. This was something that greatly fascinated her.

Mira had always wanted to spread her wings, but she believed that the repressive environment in which she had grown up, had clipped them. Her tyrannical father had never stopped her from soaring high in the field of education, but had never allowed Mira to take flight as an individual. The restless spirit inside her took flight for the first time when she found love. Thereafter, her beloved helped her to continue her flight, in spite of the shackles and ceilings. Veer had given her only a small nudge, wanting to see her spread her wings and achieve flight. The same nudge was what had caught her attention, as she watched one of the strange birds inspiring the others to face the danger, overcome it and take flight.

Naturally, the first step towards flight involved facing danger, the height of a cliff or the steepness of a slope, no matter which form it took.

These walks in the woods, watching these birds acquire the ability to fly, had become a cherished part of Mira's routine over the past decade. She was not only reminded of her lost love, but was also compelled to speculate on what could have given impetus to these birds to achieve such a feat. It made her want to improve her state of existence, making her fight loneliness and despair without him by her side.

Almost an hour had passed and Mira had to return home, but her pace was more relaxed now, partly because she was tired, and partly because the journey back was downhill. It took her hardly fifteen minutes to reach home, climb up the steep hill-cut steps and reach her front gate. Before going back into the house to get ready for the day, she paused to look at her mini-garden.

Though she had a gardener, Manjhi Bhaiya, the kind, soft-spoken man, who looked after her plants, drove her to work when she didn't want to walk, and had helped her decorate her home, she preferred to have a simple, modest garden, because the scenic beauty and innocence of Pelling was enough to soothe her inside out.

Mira observed every nuance of her garden which, perhaps, was not so 'minimal', after all. In spatial terms, it harboured a huge lawn, large enough to host a party, replete with velvet green grass and a three-seat garden swing standing in one corner, facing the entrance diagonally. This swing was one of Mira's favourite places because it was while sitting on it, enjoying the rarely sunny winters of Pelling, that Mira had finally been able to give words to the emotional rush inside her. Words that had culminated in a beautiful book, which she had published six months ago. She had published it, not for everyone to read, rather, in the hope that Veer would. She wanted him to know that she was fine, wherever she was.

In spite of their separation, in spite of the fact that

she had not allowed anyone, not even him to reach out to her, she had always known, in her heart, how tough it had been for him to let her go. She had wanted to relieve him of his burden, the guilt of knowing he was responsible for her leaving. It had taken her four years to put the book together. She had called it *The Story of Her Life*, and she had sent it out into the world to let him know that she was alive somewhere, and that he could continue with his life, separate from her, without worrying about her.

Mira's garden space also contained four silver oak trees, one in each corner, which, according to her were the most beautiful ornaments of her house. These oak trees stood out from the others in her vicinity. They looked spectacular against the backdrop of snow covered mountains and the dissolving sun. They were special not only because of how ethereal they seemed at times of snowfall, when they shone as if studded with diamonds, but also because of their extraordinary height.

If Mira stood at the foot of these trees and looked up, tracing their length through her gaze, it was hard to tell where the tree ended, as it ran continuously into the sky. It made her feel that Man was essentially so miniscule, so small, and so puny in comparison to the resplendence of nature. How ironic it was, she often thought, that man hoped to conquer all of the Earth and the universe, when he was nothing but a small part of creation, just like other animals and plants. This was one thought that often made her speculate that she too was part of that imbecile race of beings, who dreamt of conquering the whole of creation. She wondered what would have happened, had we all continued to exist in our most primal state. Human life would have been so simple, and worth living. When no other entity of nature had altered its way of life, be it the smallest grass or the largest elephant, why did man have to stick his head in the mechanism of nature and try to alter everything? Man was such a selfish being.

It was Koicha who interrupted Mira's train of thought as she came out into the garden with a cup of hot Bourn vita milk for her. Somehow Mira had not got over this childhood habit of hers, being not much of a tea or a coffee person. One cup of Bourn vita milk in the morning was her daily dose of hot drinks.

"Here," said Koicha, handing the hot cup to her, "little champ!" she continued mockingly.

Mira returned her smile with a poker face, "Very funny," she said. "What's the time?"

"9:00 a.m." Koicha replied, "and you're late."

Mira had never adopted the habit of being punctual. She was late for everything. It was almost a ritual, even if it was only five minutes, the inadvertent delay was inevitable. She didn't enjoy being late, it was just a habitual error that she couldn't seem to evade.

She looked up at Koicha, wide eyed, trying to look furious, "And you have made this milk so hot!" she said. "It's going to take me ages to drink it, or I will burn my mouth!"

Koicha knew it wasn't meant as a reprimand and gave a sarcastic sorry in return. Mira finished her milk and hurried back into the house to get ready for her morning lecture.

CHAPTER THREE

Mira stood in the bathroom, staring at her half naked reflection in the full length mirror on the opposite wall. Her mind kept wandering back to her morning's dream as she mechanically removed her clothes to take a bath.

Why had she seen his face? Why today? When over the last seven years that dream had always left her restless and confused. She had never been able to bring herself to see the dark shadowy figure properly, though she had known all along that it was Veer. But there was no avoiding it now. The confirmation of his identity had affected her deeply and she found herself wishing for the dream to come true.

A gust of cold wind and resulting goose bumps brought her back to reality and she came to terms with her un-apparelled body with its hair standing on its edges, in the reflection. Having been reared in literature, there was nothing taboo for Mira about looking at her body. She believed that one's body was the first identity of oneself – even before one's name. She had purposefully installed a full length mirror in her bathroom so that she could look at herself at least once a day, attempting to reconnect to that primary identity.

Today, however, her gaze was not of self-discovery, affirmment or scrutiny, but was blurred by the hangover of the dream. It was Veer's essence that veiled her gaze.

After all this time, she wanted to see herself the way he had seen her. The way he had looked at her, almost looking into her very soul, each time, before making love to her. The way he had devoured her with his gaze and the way he had made her blush with each movement of his eyes, his breath, gaining momentum as he drank in the sight of her, driven by raging passions. She remembered how his eyes had rested on her face, on the petite, arched bow lips that had, so often, crushed against his own, his tongue forcing its way through to to reach hers, and that soft tingling sensation as their tongues played out their dalliance, gently teasing each whilst, at the same time, deeply feeling each other's wants.

Her gaze moved down to her neck and she could feel his soft lips and his hot breath there. His breath had always been enough to ignite her sensuality, and the way his lips and tongue had played their way down to her shoulders, especially when he held her from behind, their bodies pressed together, his arms clasped firmly around her waist.

Those arms had been a great cause of speculation to Mira. Veer's build had never been one that called to mind hours at the gym, but his arms had been those of a sturdy, well built man. Wheat brown in colour and covered with soft slanting hair, exactly the texture and quantity that Mira preferred. She had loved to observe his arms, especially when he rode a motorbike. His arms, short but well curved palm and

31

fingers that firmly gripped the handles of his motorcycle. She would often take his arms and wrap them around her, caging herself in his embrace. It had always made her feel so secure and protected.

Mira had to tear herself away from her thoughts, as she stood unapparelled in the bathroom. A tear escaped from the corner of her eye. No. She must not think about that since she had no strength to go through it all again. She couldn't let herself go dwell on the past, not again, not now, all because of a dream. She shook herself out of her stupor, regaining control over her thoughts as she turned on the shower and avoided meeting her own gaze in the mirror.

Why was it still so hard for her to not think of Veer, even after eleven years? Why could she not detach herself from her memories of him, his love, and his soul? Why could she feel his touch in the water that trickled down from her shoulders to her waist? Why could she feel his breath in the wind that brushed against the nape of her neck? These questions and the subsequent passions clamoured inside, making it hard for her to disconnect. But she had to.

Mira reached out for the towel to get done with the shower and this endless reverie, but her eyes fell back on her reflection in the mirror which was now hidden behind a film of mist that had developed because of the hot water. She cleared the mist from the mirror with one hand, wanting to hide nothing from her eyes.

The curves and bends of her body that had once been traced by his breath, the inner linings and folds of her basket throbbing against her skin, the way they did each time Veer entered her. She could smell his fragrance – his favourite cream and his hair mask, the fruity smell of his face mixed with the heat of the moment and the scent of her shampoo lingering in between. The way he held her close to his body, all the while ensuring her comfort even when visiting the gardens of love that lay inside her flesh, and his pen forcing its way through the cartridge of her body and spilling its contents not over her, but inside her.

'Will you marry me?'

These were the only words that ever escaped his lips at the moment of their union and Mira, hypnotized by the awareness of such love, had only managed to blush, her breathing heavy, and bring her lips close to his ear and whisper, 'Always'. They had interlocked in that state, not wanting to let go of one another, or the moment.

When Mira came back to her senses, she had the towel in her hand and her eyes were brimming with tears, obscuring her reflection once again. She closed her eyes to settle with reality.

"I love you," her lips quivered, "Please, come back to me."

Fresh floods of tears escaped her and Mira sank to the floor. She sat still for a while, her legs held to her body, knees touching her neck, as she grieved over those moments she would never have again.

There was a gentle knock on the door, a subtle tap. "It's time," said Koicha, from the other side of the door.

Mira gathered herself and stood up. "I'm okay," she

said, wrapping the towel around her and unlocking the door. She stepped out into her bedroom without once looking back at Koicha.

There was an unusual sense of understanding between the two women and it had developed into a special bond. Koicha was the only person, besides Mira's family, who knew what had happened between him and her. Still, Koicha was secretly hopeful that her *Saheb* would one day come home to her *Didi*. She left the room without another word, but Mira knew that Koicha understood her feelings. She could sense it.

Mira got dressed for her daily lecture at the college. She put on a pastel pink high-necked sweater, blue trousers and a black overcoat. As the day was pleasant and sunny enough for it, she slipped into her favourite pair of stilettos and went down to the dining room, her hair still damp and loose. She would let it dry while she ate breakfast.

It was only as Mira was leaving that Koicha broke the silence that had settled as they ate breakfast together.

"Take care," she said, "I'll be right here." She pressed Mira's hand softly.

Mira could only smile in return as she struggled to hold back tears.

CHAPTER FOUR

It was one of those rare days when Mira found it difficult to teach at the university because Veer, his thoughts, and his memories had completely enveloped her, blocking all sources of light and peace.

Even her students could sense that there was something wrong with her. No one knew that this strong lady, who was the epitome of a good literature lecture for them, was struggling inside with a turmoil that was endless and persistent. Her eyes that always bore a certain kind of sadness and emptiness had gained further depth today.

Mira wrapped up her lecture fifteen minutes before the stipulated time, something she rarely did but today was different. She couldn't do further injustice to her students by being disloyal to them while teaching. Her thoughts were enmeshed into each other, and she needed time to think, to reflect on how long she was going to live her life this way. How long was she going to wait for him, and how long was she going to wreathe in inner conflict and yearning.

Mira gathered her thoughts and emotions as she

gathered all her books and papers from the desk, packed them in her bag and walked out of the lecture hall, towards the exit gate. She would cancel all classes for the day and spend time alone. She didn't call Manjhi Bhaiya to drive her around Pelling as she thought walking up to her destination would be better. But, walking in stilettos? She took them off and carried them in one hand as she walked barefoot away from the university.

A car was coming towards her from the opposite side, but Mira hardly noticed it, she kept walking. The car, a blue Swift Dezire, pulled over at the other side of the road and a middle aged man stepped out, dressed in blue jeans and a black pullover, carrying his coat in his hands. He was a native of Sikkim and taught Mathematics at the same university as Mira. He had once proposed marriage to her and, although everyone had thought it an appropriate match, she had, of course refused him. She had been furious with him for even thinking of it. She felt that her soul, which had been piously in possession of the man she loved, had been infiltrated by this other man, who meant nothing to her.

"Mira!" that man called out from behind, "Professor Mira?" but, she didn't care to respond even though she could hear her name being called out faintly. She kept walking, her mind empty as a new slate.

He overtook her and stood in front of her smiling his crooked smile, his eyes further squinted because of the bright sun.

"Aseem," she said slowly, recognizing his face from the chaos that her mind harboured at that moment, and coming to terms with reality. "Hi, Aseem" she said, trying to sound cheerful.

"Hey, what's the matter?" he asked directly, looking straight at her face trying to read something. She looked drained and for the first time he noticed age on Mira's face or maybe it was just her demeanour all shrivelled up, "You look awful."

"No, I'm fine," she said, looking at him, indifferently.

"Sure?" he asked, concern dripping from his face. She nodded with a subtle smile in reply to him. "Leaving so early?" he continued with his interrogation.

"Yes. I don't feel like teaching today," after a short pause, she added, "Aseem, I'm in a hurry, I'll get back to you tomorrow," as she cut him short, wanting to escape from any human presence.

"Yeah, sure," he muttered, seemingly irritated, but he regained cheerfulness as he continued, "Well Mira, I just thought I'd share something personal with you," as he looked intently at her while speaking, pausing for her reaction, but when she gave none, he chose her silence as a cue to continue, "I'm getting married," he stated abruptly but cheerfully.

Even though Mira was not very fond of him, she was still happy to hear the news of his marriage as a colleague would and should. She gave him a warm smile, "Congratulations Dr. Aseem", she said, wanting to introduce a formal tone to her voice.

"Thank you," he replied, beaming with joy, "but plain congratulations won't work, you will have to come to my wedding as well," he entreated. Without giving her a moment to speak, he continued with his rhapsody, "I'll let you know the date and venue once I have the wedding cards ready," he said it all at once.

Though Aseem was nearing forty years of age, he still had the spirit of a twenty year old and he believed in living life to contentment, not how Mira chose to live her life.

"I'm really happy for you," she told him, "God bless. I'll surely try and catch up with your wedding," she spoke, quietly and at ease.

"Okay then, see you later!" he said and walked off towards his car.

Mira was left smiling to herself as she continued walking towards her destination. It was a smile of happiness and self contempt. She was so speculative about everything. It seemed to her as if her life had stopped and, indeed, it had. The promise she had made to her twenty-six year old self had, inadvertently, been broken. To fight away her negative feelings, Mira had thrown herself into her writing, but even after one successful book, those memories and thoughts continued to haunt her. The void had not left, nor had it been filled.

Not once, in eleven years, had Mira thought of moving on. She couldn't. It would have been a betrayal of her love for Veer. Her feelings for him had been too real, too pure, and she had made a vow to herself that she would never tarnish herself that way. She would never let him get the better of it. She would wait for him, even though she knew he would never return. Though their predicament had been brought on by Fate, it had been he who had fallen prey, had proved too weak to fight for their future. She would never allow herself to be weak. It was her way of tormenting, as well as loving him, all these years. But, in truth, no other man had appealed to her, and no woman either. Mira felt she had become sensually inert. The only times she felt anything in that way was when he returned to haunt her thoughts.

Today was one of those days and she knew nothing lay ahead of her but tears and torment.

Mira reached the ridge she had been heading for. She often came here, after class, to watch the sun set. But today was different. It was different because she had come to re-live her past and to reflect on her present.

The future was beyond the scope of speculation. It had been hopeful for the past eleven years.

CHAPTER FIVE

The ridge was not a special garden or a café or any other place with historical or aesthetic importance in the records of Sikkim, rather it was just another side of the hill, but it was an extremely picturesque view if you considered it through Mira's eyes. It was a place she had often visited in the past and it had stored a reservoir of her tears, her memories, her sighs and her experiences in its vast openness. It was as if she had lived a part of her life in that space and it calmed her, offering her solace directly from nature's lap, each time she came begging for it.

There were days when she would spend hours sitting down on the wild grass, as soft as velvet, and run her hands over it, feeling its cold wetness as the aroma of melted snow made its way inside her partly through scent and partly through touch.

The walk from the university to that spot was considerable, but Mira had covered it without much pain. She had been engrossed in her thoughts and the journey was downhill.

There are times in life when your mind gets stuck on

one thing while your body is involved in some other activity and you never realize how this transition takes place and the moment you come to terms with acknowledging this shift, you're back to your real thoughts, back to what your hands were busy doing or back to where you were standing. Smaller versions of such trances happen when you wake up out of it and realize that you had been staring constantly at a person for quite long, making him/her uncomfortable in the process, but your thoughts were not focused on them but rather at some other place or time.

Pain has the power to extend this short reverie into a sustained trance. Pain being the only sublime is capable of inducing this state of semi-consciousness in a fully aware individual. Today, Mira too, had been seething with pain, not any physical pain but emotional pain – the kind that shreds a person from inside and destroys their senses to make them numb to external forces.

When she reached the destined location, she looked around, almost dazed by the bright sun whose rays were warm and pleasant. She observed that beautiful place, slowly coming back to her senses as she felt an abundance overpowering her. She wanted to reach out to that higher entity. "Make me a part of you," she whispered, carefully letting go of each word as if they were being recorded by some mystical force, each word escaping as distinctly as beads from the grasp of a priest chanting prayers. But her words were not uttered in a prayer, they were words of surrender after a lost battle.

She allowed the over-arching Nature to overcome her fears, but the human mind is inherently wicked and it keeps engaging with the negativities that after a

41

certain point we tend to avoid solutions to our problems. The same thing had happened with Mira. No matter how much she tried to break the shackles of the past by distancing herself physically, her mind kept attaching itself back to it.

Mira tried to remember the last time she visited this place, asking for liberation from her suffering. It must have been a few months ago, maybe a year. She had been troubled because her parents wanted her to come home, to be at her brother's wedding. They had wanted her to meet someone – a divorcee, who was apparently a good man and had suffered a past similar to her own, as his wife had run away with her lover. For some reason, her parents had insisted on her meeting this man because they felt that he would be a good match for her. But his past was nothing like hers.

Mira's past was not one of betrayal, only of cowardice and duty. She had been upset to hear her mother speak the way the others did because she knew the whole story, but, after spending endless hours and tears at that ridge, she had understood her parents' sudden desire to find a suitable match for her, after so many years.

"We just want to see you happy," her mother had said over the phone, her voice choked when unable to sustain in front of her daughter's stubbornness.

What her father had once said to her also made sense somehow, "You know Mira when after a certain age, you will look back at your life, you will hate yourself for not loving yourself enough," he had written to her in an email, to which she had never been able to reply.

Even though her last pilgrimage to the ridge had helped her to see her parents' perspective, they had, for some reason or another, stopped pressuring her. Nothing certain had come out of the meditation on the ridge, she had only continued with her usual routine of writing, reading and teaching at the university.

Today, however, this place seemed different, almost hopeful. She could sense an unknown energy in the air and she felt that today was going to be the deciding day of her life when, perhaps, she would finally be able to let go of the past. She had no clue why she felt a strange energy in that place.

She stood at the edge of the road and devoured the scenic beauty of the ridge with her eyes, ears and nose. Her knee brushed against the broken railings, which had originally been installed to protect vehicles and people from crossing over, but were now used mainly as a bench by young lovers, seeking to have some romance on the roadside. Mira guessed that some speeding vehicle must have broken the railings a long time ago. "How similar are our roles in life," she uttered softly, touching the railings with her fingers before stepping onto the grass that lay beyond them. The wet grass tickled her feet and a current shot upwards within her as the majesty of nature initiated its effect on her. She sat down on the grass and removed her coat, the sun was warm enough, she thought. Mira placed her stilettos on her right, at a distance.

The hill on which she sat had a great height, but it wasn't a steep hill. One could easily stand, sit or even walk down it, with measured steps. Facing it were a number of mountain ranges, snow-peaked at this time of year. From the place where she sat, Mira could relish not only the beauty and serenity of nature, but could also smell the peculiar fragrance of the hills – the smell of melting snow mixed with the aroma of mountainous soil. She could hear the gurgling murmur of the stream that flowed between her hill and the mountains opposite and, although Mira was at a considerable height, she could hear the waves striking against the rocks, creating a huge uproar that reverberated through the valley like lightning, especially at a time when the snow was melting and the flow of the stream was fast paced. There were tiny houses on either side of that stream, belonging to the poorest of them with dilapidated huts and mud walls.

The breeze stroked across her face, playing with loose strands of her hair with it and bringing small twigs and leaves dancing towards her. It brought her a dried oak leaf, one that glittered in the bright sunlight. It flapped and wheeled about her with the force of the breeze. She caught hold of it by its tail and, observing the intricate design it bore in the shape of carved out edges, she thought of how free and detached it was. She longed to be an inanimate object with no thoughts in her head, she longed to be like that free oak leaf in her hand, the little oak leaf that was going to act as a totem for her and which, by the end of her soiree in that place, would bear the full burden of her past.

Her attention shifted to the innumerable rows of death flags in Sikkim, another fascination of that quiet and alienated state of India. The death flags were planted by the natives of Sikkim at the death of their family members, and their number always seemed to surpass that of the living men and women of the region. This forced Mira to speculate on death. It was a familiar subject. Even when she was young,

44

she had often contemplated suicide over the problems she faced at the time, problems which now seemed menial to her. But no matter how bad things had seemed, she had never been able to put her contemplations into action. She understood that death was more certain than life, but she also believed that life couldn't end just by wanting it to. For her, even those who were successful in taking their own lives were directed by a higher power to do so. Mira wondered why this higher power had never turned its will to her.

She checked herself before delving deeper into the topic of death. She had come here for another reason, to let go of the passions that had built inside her that morning, to cry her heart out, to pity how miserable her life had become, and to contemplate the oblivion she was heading towards. Self-pity had once been her primary emotion. But then, of course, Veer had made way into her life, and it had become a dream. A dream she had never thought would come to such an abrupt end and that life would give her a reason to exist miserably for the rest of her time.

With that oak leaf twirling in her hand and the beautiful scene soothing her soul, Mira plunged into a journey of the past where there lay many unanswered questions and many parts of her life awaiting redefinition.

NEW DELHI

CHAPTER SIX

Mira, traditional yet contemporary, just like her name, was a twenty-one year old twenty-first century woman. She was soft in her comportment and dressing, but a wildfire inside. To be precise, she was like a time bomb, never quite exploding, but the ticking was constant, perpetually waiting for the right moment, not to destroy everything around her in the explosion, but to make her existence worthwhile.

Dressed to subtlety in a white *kurti* and pink leggings along with an ethnic waistcoat, she wore small *jhumkis* in her ears and her hair was pulled back in a semi-parting, with two sections, from behind her ears, pinned back with the versatile bobby pins.

She stood at the metro station waiting for the next train. She was returning home from college, a copy of Margaret Mitchell's *Gone with the Wind* clutched in her hand. Mira's face was small and oval with a petite nose. Her nose often worked as a cynosure on her face, not because of its domineering presence, rather because of its understated appearance. Her

47

eyes were small and her cheekbones well formed, adorned with at least one pimple mark, or with the pimple itself. Mira had hated acne on her face when she was in her teens but, with time, she had learnt not to be bothered by it. Her eyes were lined with a hint of kohl and her lips were painted pink with a subtle gloss.

Mira's life had been simple, very simple. In fact, it had been simple to the extent of boredom, because she had learned to conform to the external fetters in her life that caged her individuality, hindering her from soaring up into the limitless sky towards an infinite existence. However, there was something about Mira that not everyone knew, that she was a wild soul inside. She knew that on the inside she burnt a like raging fire, similar to the flame of a lamp when it is simpering and flickering because of the moistened wick.

There was only one soul who could save that fire from being extinguished and, in the process, push her to flap out her wings, jump over the edge and take flight. This man, Veer, came into Mira's life to liberate her from her mental shackles, and to teach her the correct and simplest way of living life – contentedly.

Mira had often been suicidal in the first twenty years of her existence. She had often thought of death as the ultimate liberator from pain and suffering, a final escape from her mind forged miseries, but, in all these years, she had never been able to take that final step. The speculations had only been in her mind and she didn't know if she would ever be able to put her thoughts into action. The thoughts, however, had receded over time, not because God had chosen to press the 'Reset' button on Mira's life, but because love had come into her life enmeshing her within its folds, first with reluctance and gradually all at once.

Veer was the soul to gather the bits and pieces of Mira's shattered self and hold them together. Ever since their first utterance of love for each other, he had been that healing touch that made her realise her true potential, had shown her inner strengths and given her a reason to live happily. This man was not some sturdy, good looking man, godlike in appearance, rather he was an average looking person who had one perfect feature – he brought tears of joy and a radiant smile to those who thought of him.

Veer had short but straight hair, always brushed in a peculiar twisted fashion, bending slightly towards the left, and bushy black eyebrows that arched over his big, black eyes. His nose resembled the Indian snack called the pakora, as it quivered at times and his lips, formed to perfection and as smooth as a newborn child's – pink and supple as if glossed with a permanent lip balm. Average in size and height and lean in build, he wore very simple clothes – a plain white Kurta-shirt maybe, blue jeans teamed with his favourite pair of 'Crocs'. He was such a brand conscious person yet so simple to the core. Behind the short beard that covered half of his face, he had extraordinary glowing skin, almost an angelic radiance, surreal and pleasing to the eyes.

A versatile personality with vivid inputs to the art of living a happy life, Veer strived not for any remarkable educational degree or for truckloads of money, but for love and happy relationships. He was the one to teach Mira the real meaning of her life, a life that was beyond the everyday pretences and vain enterprises, a life that made her 'live' and not just breathe, a life that made her dance her heart out and a life that prioritized love above everything else.

Love, not in the man and woman sense, exclusively, though that was the first love she experienced through him and for him, but love across horizons, extending to the people around her and acknowledging the beauty of things around her. It was as if he had opened her senses to perceive, touch, feel and smell life.

But there was another man in Mira's life – her father. An authoritarian, didactic human being, and a person she abhorred yet cared for at the same time. The tragedy of this father – daughter relationship was that Mira never really got a chance to connect with her father as she deserved to, not because she chose to turn away, but because her father chose to maintain a distance. A distance that widened with each passing year, each passing moment, and almost each passing breath of their existence.

Her father was two people trapped in one body, or so it often seemed – a short-tempered, rude and self-centred person on one hand, and a jovial light-hearted person on the other. These contradictory personas of her father made it hard for Mira to give any true thought to her feelings about him and, with time, she learnt to conform to the situation. As long as one could abide by his rules and ideals, there would be no problem, but the moment he sensed one thought of rebellion, they were in for trouble.

Mira was generally a jovial and light-hearted person. She would never wish to break anyone's heart, yet her heart broke because of her father. A cynical, hypocritical and orthodox IAS officer who wished to control his daughter as though with a whip, but, often, a soul tormented with a whip grows strong enough to break that whip into two.

She was reared in an atmosphere where there was no shortage of food, money or material things, but the only things that were lacking were love, respect, understanding and, most importantly, free will.

Though her father never once stopped her from studying or from pursuing a higher education, nor did he impose marriage upon her from an early age, still she harboured a feeling of resentment towards him, because he wanted to clip her flight as an individual. This was why Mira constantly sought salvation, at times in literature and at times in writing. But true salvation never came until she met Veer, the love of her life, who gave her the courage to flap out her wings, those that were already there but only bound with a whip. Once freed, those wings let her soar up into the sky, with him by her side.

CHAPTER SEVEN

In Mira's family, one never heard expressions of love being made to one another. Of course they loved each other, but they never expressed it. But then, that is how many Indian families functioned – on underlying notions of love, and her family was no exception to this. She often thought it would have been better if the four members of their family lived in the four separate corners of the country and met only four times a year. This was something that Mira had sometimes suggested to her mother when they had such discussions. Her mother would only end up laughing at the idea.

The one person who kept them all together in the same house, and not in four separate corners of the country, was the woman of the house – the wife, the mother and friend. Mira's mother was a very different kind of a human being, a kind hardly manufactured on Earth these days. She was such that Mira never aspired to be like her.

It wasn't that her mother didn't look after the family or didn't behave properly, as a mother ought to, or because she was like the mothers from those soap operas, always scheming against people. No, it was simply that her mother was the epitome of love, keeping the family glued together in spite of the many cracks it had. Mira would never be like her mother, not because she looked down on her, but because she could never raise herself to such high standards of familial devotion. She was no superhuman or saint, but a simple doctor by profession who derived great pleasure out of healing her patients. She was famous in the neighbourhood for her accurate diagnosis and she could always tell, just by the looks on the faces of her children when there was something wrong with them. Mira suspected this was something all mothers could do, but still, her mother was special.

She was a pious soul and always working on or worried about losing weight. For as long as she could remember, Mira had always seen her mother attempting, in vain, to lose weight. Only once had her mother been able to shed a considerable amount of weight, around ten to fifteen kilograms, but that was a long time ago, when Mira was around eleven or twelve. She only had a faint memory of her mother looking extraordinarily pretty in a blue and green chiffon sari as she got into the car, and put her seatbelt on, exclaiming, "Oh, it buckled completely for the first time!" She seemed so happy and content in Mira's memory.

Mira absolutely loved her mother. She was her lifeline and only confidante, besides her younger sister Ananya. But, for some reason, she had never been able to completely spell out her heart to her mother, either for fear of hurting her feelings or for fear of her father. She had never told her mother how she had bunked college to go and watch a movie with friends or to go out dancing with them. Though she had always had an aversion to drinking and similar activities, like smoking and taking drugs, because of her father's habit.

However, Mira had tried all sorts of alcohol. Initially, she had been attracted to the idea of it, but then, after a month or two, she had grown sick of the smell and the after-effects of being drunk.

Once, she had got as drunk as a mouse, and had spent an entire evening with Veer, on the steps of the parking lot, at the mall and he had helped her clean herself after numerous bouts of belching, waiting patiently for her to come back to her senses. That night she had realised the wrong she had done in driving herself into the snares of alcohol abuse. She had no right to make him suffer the way her mother had suffered after marrying her father. Moreover, she didn't want to feel herself to be weak or evil in her mother's eyes by behaving in such an awful manner.

The only positive thing that had come out of this experience was that Mira had developed an awareness of the smell and taste of alcohol, so she would never be fooled by anyone into accidently consuming it spiked in a soft drink. Delhi was the place for girls to know about such instances when spiking drinks was as common as eating pizza, especially if you were a girl out at a party with your friends. Cigarettes and drugs were out of the question. Mira hated the idea of losing one's health for a short trip or trance, the way many of her peers were doing.

Only for one person had Mira led a dual life. No matter how much she had wanted to tell her mother about him she hadn't been able to. She had known that there would come a time when her mother would need to understand, but that time was to be somewhere in the future. For now, her love for her mother's would be overpowered by her fear of her father.

Mira's mother loved her children unconditionally, but Mira knew she loved their father more than them. Mira had never been able to understand this kind of love, where one person was fatally striving to put their heart, their soul, and even their blood into a relationship, whereas the other person was concerned only with taking everything and giving back nothing. It had always been the same old story in Mira's home – her father and mother would have a tiff over something trivial. Her father would shout abuses at her mother and, at times, indulge in violence. Her mother too would shout and scream out her lungs in retaliation, and the children would try to intervene, crying and begging them to stop and, eventually, after a many tears, discussions and rounds of the blame game, they would all go back to sleep. Mira's mother would then try very hard to avoid any communication with her husband, even moving out of their bedroom and sleeping with the children for the subsequent two to three days, sometimes even a week, but she would give in to her husband at the slightest apology or request for reconciliation.

*

Mira had a younger sister, Ananya and a brother, Aditya, the youngest in the family. She shared a close bond with both of them. In a household that was constantly disintegrating, these children had consolidated their relationships in order to prevent the family from falling apart. Mira had later learnt that this was what generally happened in broken homes, where the adults were oblivious to their responsibilities and the little ones took up the duty of holding the family together. It was funny how, in a family of five people, one person had been capable of meddling in the lives of the other four enough, making them suffer and believe that their family was, indeed, a broken one.

Mira had grown so averse to alcohol, watching her father come home drunk and hearing him howling, shouting abuse, and kicking the young ones around, that she had decided never to marry a man who even touched such glittering liquids. It was absolute luck that Mira found such a man, a soul untouched by even a drop of alcohol or other 'family-destroying agent'. This was one impeccable quality in him, developed without any compulsion or any conditioning from his family. He had never been attracted to such things, be it alcohol or drugs or even smoking, in his twenty-six years and he never would be. For Mira, he seemed to be a customized gift from God, who had wrapped this pious soul in a human body for her sake only.

Mira knew she could never be as perfect. Her father had reminded her often enough. The whole family was always found lacking in perfection by the alcoholic and self obsessed father, no matter how hard they tried to please him, first their mother, initially as his wife, and then as the mother of his children, then his daughters and, finally, his son.

"I have strived hard in the sun, in my village, without money, without food, no air conditioner and look where I stand today. Here I am posted in the capital of the country, and I came from a menial village, but today I serve at the most prestigious post of the

56

nation, and you, are you *my* children, *my* blood?" her father roared one night at his trembling children, long before they had learnt to throw his stones and filth back at him, "and look at you, not capable of even being a sweeper with 89% marks and a plain graduation degree and now you want to do masters but not IAS? I employ sweepers and peons at my office who hold masters in science and other subjects. It seems that I will have to be ashamed of myself because of the kind of children I have produced," he rattled on.

His wife, all the while, sat pale-faced looking at her children with sorry eyes. She knew they were brilliant young children with a good academic record and with good values that she had instilled in them – always respectful towards their elders and caring towards their fellow beings. Not once had they done anything bad or shameful.

At times, Mira wondered whether her father did this on purpose, if he humiliated everyone to maintain his power and stay, as always, the head of the family, but not the father figure, because, inherently, he knew that he was in the wrong that he didn't deserve such a loving family. Mira suspected that his ego made him undervalue them, so that they would always remain cowed under his thumb.

"What kind of children have you produced? You selfish woman, do you not know how to bring up kids decently?" he roared at his wife, moving towards her.

Slap.

Everybody was silent. The children were so angry that they wished to kill him in that moment. Yes, kill him. This feeling arose in them many times in the past and they had thought of harming their father physically, in order to put an end to all their traumas and suffering. They wanted to avenge their distorted childhood, full of images of drunkenness and physical violence, towards themselves and towards their mother.

There had been times when their neighbours had sent for the police, complaining of disturbances." Mira had seen her mother recoiling from her father inside the house and, then, putting up a façade to answer the door to the police inspectors, asking them to go away. Mira had wanted to scream out to them that nothing, absolutely nothing, was all right. She wanted them to take her father away and imprison him forever, because he, and only he, was responsible for their rotten existence – he and his bottles of alcohol. But, of course, this wish of hers was never granted.

Even though Mira loved her mother dearly, she was also hurt and disappointed in her, there also festered a little resentment in her mind, for her mother being a selfish coward. The fact that her mother had continued to live this way, dragging her children into such a furious and filthy life, exposing their innocent childhoods into such a dysfunctional family, angered Mira deeply.

Why had she not put an end to all this? Why had she allowed her children to suffer in this way, trapping them in this prison-house, where they were not free to go where they wanted to, meet their friends and family as they wished to, and wear the clothes they wanted to, or even study the subjects they chose to? Mira, being the eldest, was the most affected by this anger and, that particular day, she felt a burst of courage swelling inside her, reprimanding her for allowing all the injustices in the house. She would not sit and cry over her predicament any longer, nor would she listen to the abuse thrown at them by their remorseless father.

She stood up, wiped away the tears streaming from her red eyes and ran to position herself, as a wall, in front of her mother – protecting her mother and defying her father in a single act, an act committed by a nineteen year old girl, who had inadvertently stepped into adulthood way before her time.

The younger siblings stood terrified, 'Oh, what had their sister done today?' Their thoughts were clear in their eyes and their faces spoke of fear, but Mira had acquired a new strength and she stood, fearlessly, between her mother and the man who was her father.

"Don't you dare," she growled at him between her tears, her voice choked and barely audible. But she had said it. Naturally, her father was shocked – shocked at the audacity of this young girl, who dared to speak to him in that manner. He was the 'head of the family' and he couldn't allow such rebellion to take root. Of course, he wasn't aware that the seeds of rebellion had already been sowed in the three other souls present in that dingy oppressive room. This time, it was Mira, who took the blows, instead of her mother, but she did not budge from her place. He tried to push her away, to reach the woman standing behind her, but she stood sturdy in her place, her face red and fire in her eyes.

"Over my dead body," she scowled at him, meeting his gaze, fierce and unmoved. There had been enough of his whip and, that day, Mira had broken his whip in two.

Her father, however, was not to be subdued so easily, he had to shout, roar and create an environment of repression and fear, so he shouted at her, this time louder. He called Mira and her mother whores, humiliated Mira for not clearing her medical entrances, called her incompetent, called the other children failures as well, broke the glass, threw away the food and stormed out of the room.

Nevertheless, Mira stood undaunted in her act. For the first time in her life, she felt satisfied with herself. She had fought her greatest fear. She was proud of herself. The four of them slept together in the children's room, crying and consoling each other, but also supporting the eldest sister in the new stand that she had taken.

It was that night Mira realised her actions had been spurred by something, Veer had said to her, when she had spilled out the darkest of her family's secrets to him.

"God helps those who help themselves," he had said, with a small smile.

Mira closed her tear filled eyes to sleep, and realised that she understood his meaning, and she slept with a readiness to face this changing facet of her existence.

CHAPTER EIGHT

Love had various nuances for a nineteen year old Mira and the most visible relationship available to her for scrutiny, was that of her parents. Of course not a very suitable example to study love and, at that age, it was very hard for her to tell whether there existed any kind of a love between her parents, because she had never witnessed any expression of love being made between them, in any form whatsoever. She was biased towards sensing attachment on her mother's side, but, no matter how hard she looked, she rarely saw any from her father.

Now, whether this affection she sensed from her mother could be termed as love, or not, was a subject of much debate for the young girl, as her sensibilities took shape along with her body. As a teenager, she believed she knew that there was no love between her parents and she ardently wished them to divorce each other. It was only later, when she began to understand the intricacies of the magic called love, and the subtleties of such partnerships, through her own relationship with him, that she was able to observe the love between her mother and father.

Gradually, she noticed love, not only from her mother, but also from her father. She realised that they cared about each other. She could sense the

61

mutual care that went into a husband-wife relationship. She realised that every relationship had its own decorum and décor, meaning that every relationship functioned on its own set of ideals and was projected to others in its own peculiar way. And that she had no right to judge on the basis of what she perceived on the surface.

Even if Mira's parents were not very verbose regarding their expressions of love, she could sense her father getting upset if her mother was not well, or when she faced certain problems regarding her work. She could see him missing his wife if whenever her mother went on short trips to her maternal home. She could sense her mother struggling to sleep properly at night because her husband was out of town and that made her restless. She could see her mother avoiding dinner, or eating stale food, because there wouldn't be enough left for her father to have.

Whether these feelings had been present before Mira had her own experience of love or whether they only began afterwards, was something she couldn't quite decide.

As a young teenager, Mira had been against the concept of marriage, possibly after witnessing the tumultuous relationship between her parents, but with time, she had learned to sense the warmth of love in marriages, both those formed through love and those that were arranged. She'd even learnt to see the warmth in her parents' marriage. Indian marriages, she had initially believed, were made solely to torture the husband and the wife, where each was tied together by the shackles of society and tradition, but this belief of hers gradually diminished as she began to look at marriages with a fresh perspective.

62

By the time she was twenty-one, she was able to pick up the graces and faults in most of the marriages she encountered. Even though she always used to tease her mother, saying "I'm never going to get married. Who would want to ruin their life to be a lifelong slave to someone?" in her heart, she knew that marriage was a sacrosanct relationship – sacred and sanctified, not by any external agency, but by the two souls involved. For her, it was the union of the souls that mattered, something that had been achieved already in case of her relationship with Veer.

CHAPTER NINE

*T*his world was full of sufferings and qualms and we tend to ponder over our trivial problems. How does each person make it a habit to never let stupid misgivings and inadequacies affect us, when in this world, people with much less than we have, are better at living and not just existing. Today, in the metro, I saw one such person. These instances and images of people add to the experiential richness of my life and often lead me to digressions of this sort that I am forced to pour out my heart through words.

She was both physically and somewhat mentally disabled, yet more able than I am, to pursue a normal, happy existence. Why, if she can do it, is it so hard for me, who, having been endowed with the best of faculties, has had constant complaints with life.

There she is, sitting in front of me and busily engaged in her smart phone, organising and arranging her life with more dexterity and passion than most of us. I am led to wonder how she responds to the pruning eyes of our fellow passengers, some of whom are looking down on her, as if trying to remind her of her so called

64

*defects. I tend to become self-conscious over people
staring at me, even when it is simply because I am
inappropriately dressed.   Yet here she is, radiating
confidence and love for life.*

Mira closed the notes section of her phone. This was
her usual habit. Whenever she felt a sudden surge to
record her emotions, she would put them down like
this and, later, transfer them into her writing diary
or onto her blog.

She thought of the many times she had been self-
conscious. Attire, something so superficial had
always intrigued her because she had been brought
up in an environment of strict and disciplined
clothing measures, for both boys and girls. Her
father had had the supreme command in matters of
dressing, be it for her, her sister, her mother, or for
even her brother.

The women in the family were not allowed to wear
shirts and jeans or any other forms of fashionable
dress. Ethnic and traditional were the safest option
and, that too, was limited to knee length *kurtis* with
either *salwar* or jeans. Leggings were also to be
avoided.

For her brother there were restrictions upon the kind
of jeans he wore – they must not be very tight or low-
waisted.

Of course, such things shouldn't really matter in
one's everyday life, but when you had to worry, every
single day, about what to wear to college or to work,
the constant worry about what could be indecent, in
even the slightest way would often tip you over the
edge and into frustration because you couldn't just
wear what you felt like wearing.

Though Mira liked all kinds of clothing, from short dresses to traditional *kurtis*, she inherently knew where to draw the line between the fashionable and the vulgar.

There was a surge of something called jeggings, at that point of time, and they were very popular among young girls. They were really good-fitting, body-hugging pants, made of a very flexible material that took the shape of the body too entirely. Young well-made girls wearing such pants were tolerable to Mira, though she didn't like the way these pants enhanced the vaginal area, giving it a proper V-shape. But what was further disastrous were disproportionate women thrusting themselves into these poor pants and, at the same time, teaming them with crop tops, not only enhancing their V-shaped beauty, but also forcing their curves into huge distorted mountains. People had a right to wear whatever they wanted to wear, as it is, Mira never really voiced these opinions.

She had always found it hard to understand, and come to terms with, the restrictions imposed upon her. She knew very well how to carry herself decently in all kinds of clothes without being at all vulgar. So, what reason did she have to be self conscious. She decided to learn from the extraordinary girl in the metro.

She often wondered why she often noticed such people in the metro, when other passengers seemed to deliberately ignore them, and why she was so strongly sympathetic towards them. Perhaps it was because some of her friends had not been given an equal chance in life. In college, she had a classmate who was visually impaired, but shared a great connection with everybody in the group, including the teachers. He had excellent comedic timing, a strong mimicking talent, and he could sense people through their voice. Another one had been one suffering from muscular palsy, but was such an avid reader that Mira's knowledge failed her whenever she got into a literary conversation with him.

She remembered another such experience she had had while travelling in the Delhi Metro. She had seen a young boy, eighteen to nineteen years of age and incapable of sight. The metro guard escorted him to the women's coach because that was the least crowded, and a girl, even left a seat for him, but just as he was about to sit, he stopped himself. Maybe he thought that there weren't any vacant seats.

However, Mira, in her mind, had been desperate to get him seated. Of course, she hadn't made any efforts to help him, because half the things she felt she must do, she never had the confidence to achieve. She just didn't have the courage to assert herself or, maybe, she was simply used to adapting to situations around her, rather than controlling them herself.

Mira could never bring herself to terms with accepting how such people led their lives, often making a success out of their disabilities and was often fascinated by the way these people found their own worlds to amuse themselves, a world that Mira and others like her could never understand.

CHAPTER TEN

Mira's love for Veer began like a dream, but then, each love story is no less than a dream, at least for the two people involved. That is human nature.

Our things, our love stories, and our books are always more special than those of others. Of course, Mira was no exception to this and, for her, their relationship was the most special.

They both were eighteen when they met each other for the first time. It wasn't a 'puppy' love or love at first sight, as they call it, rather it had nothing to do with love at all. It started off as friendship, a plain and simple friendship that no one expected to blossom into a full fledged romance by the end of their eighteenth year.

Mira was a shy girl, not exactly introvert but not someone who was likely to take the first step, even for friendship. She was the type who could survive a six month long language course without a single friend to talk to, and she was also the type with a large group of friends in school and college. For her, it always depended on how well she connected with the people around her. If there was no one with whom she felt a connection, she ended up having no friends at all.

Mira had joined coaching classes in Delhi to prepare for medical entrances after completing her twelfth standard. She was a no-nonsense girl on the outside, of a quiet and studious demeanour completely unaware of her inner self. She had decided that she would be strictly involved in her studies and that she would attend a top-notch medical institute in New Delhi the following year.

Little did she know what life had in store for her. What life offered to her as a gift seemed unwanted in the first place – Veer too, was one of those gifts from the universe.

The complete opposite of the soft and subtle Mira, he was a vivacious individual unhindered by the demands of the future and the shackles of the present. He had the talent of gelling well with both the genders alike and, often, there were a number of girls drooling over him. He always had enough to shower attention on each of them. He wasn't the best looking, rich and 'oh-so-sexy' type of a guy – not the one who came riding to class in an Audi, but he had a good sense of humour and wit along with decent looks.

From Shreya to Anjana to Zubeida to Harpreet to Maria, there was no end to the list of the girls who had a crush on Veer. There were very few times Mira even had a chance to interact with him, which was not much to his liking. He had a keen eye for her, but not in the same way as he paid attention to the other girls. There was something deeply intriguing about her and, little did he know, he would eventually get to swim in the deep recesses of her heart.

There were little things about Veer that brought him to Mira's keen observance. The first of which took place a week after their classes had begun.

The classrooms were unusually hot during the summers, because a room with forty to fifty students, one teacher, no fan and a faulty air conditioner was always likely to heat up like a furnace. One pedestal fan had been installed at the rear end of the room, in the hope that it would, somehow, aerate the entire room but, to everyone's dismay, the fan seemed to be non-existent. Veer was the one sitting closest to the fan, naughty and mischievous as he was, he hadn't let anyone else take that seat. After twenty minutes of a sweaty lecture by an old jiggered Chemistry teacher, Mira saw Veer pick up the pedestal fan and place it right next to the trembling and perspiring old man. He did this in spite of others harrowing him for giving up the fan, but he shut them up with a smile that had reverence for the elderly teacher.

That was the first time Mira had noticed this human being in class and she felt an unfamiliar happiness inside, that such a queer individual was better and more human than most of the intelligent students of the class, who were supposed to become doctors in life yet could not prioritise human values above their own pleasure.

The next few weeks passed with innocent smiles and looks at each other, but Veer wasn't a slow and steady type of person and, within a month of the commencement of their course, he proposed his love to Mira.

Of course, she was baffled. She had to pretend to be taken aback, surprised, even a bit shocked, but in her heart, she was bursting with joy on receiving this proposal, which she couldn't reciprocate. Not because it was Veer, who had proposed it, but because this was the first time any boy had asked her out.

In school, she had been an ordinary girl, focused on her studies and her girlfriends but not boys. Then again, she hadn't had much scope of interacting with the boys, as her parents' idea of ensuring their daughter remained safely virginal, had been to enrol her in an all-girls convent school between kindergarten and twelfth standard. Naturally, that had not left her with much latitude for falling in love, but Mira had always hoped and believed that she would fall into this oblivion. However, that it would be with a person like Veer was certainly out of the question.

The right kind of a guy for Mira, in her imagination, had always been a tall, classy gentleman with a great sense of style and, most importantly, equipped with good English diction. But here was a man who didn't need any of that to make a place for himself in Mira's heart. He won her through the purity of his soul, which was as chaste as the morning dew.

Love between them, as an emotion, developed much later. Initially, it was plain affection mingled with fascination and respect towards each other. Thereafter, their hearts gave way into this absurd feeling.

71

Veer's first proposal of love had been a trick of his overactive mind and he had really contrived a way to that situation. He had taken Mira's number from a studious friend of his, who was on talking terms with her and texted her the same evening. This was before the world was taken over by instant messaging apps and smart phones. Text messages were very much used as love letters in those days and Mira was bewildered to see an "I like you" on her square shaped phone just after two or three 'Hello – How are you?' exchanges.

However, at that point, Veer had not really meant it to the full depth of its possibility. At least, that was what he told her a year or so into their relationship.

"That was only to check your reaction," he had said to her, one evening, while they were reminiscing about their past. But, in spite of everything, that one text message had kicked off her life.

Mira was unlike the other youngsters of her generation, she wasn't orthodox, but she hadn't imbibed the irrationalities of her age. For instance, she was not the experimental kind, not like individuals who got into relationships for fun and variety, as they liked to call it. She had a place for only one man in her life and she gave her heart to him, wholly, but not as quickly as Veer had surrendered himself.

Mira took a long six months to return an answer because she had to take time, to decide, to get to know Veer and, most importantly, to fall gradually in love with him, before she could commit herself entirely. It was a promise she had made for herself that if ever she should fall in love, it would be a seal of a lifetime.

The initial days were spent blushing in class, exchanging glances and getting to know each other by talking religiously each night. It was exactly the kind of courtship that Mira had always wanted. Why Veer chose to get carried away with her old school thoughts was something she never understood.

How they used to keep looking at each other, each of them searching for the other whenever they entered the classroom, how Veer always sat near her, either in the same row or next to her in the adjacent row, and how she felt restless whenever he wasn't around. His flirtatious lines in their conversations, the sharing of their food and how everyone in the class knew that they had a 'thing' for each other, sometimes the teachers included.

Veer remained patient for those first six months of their blooming relationship, till the time she willingly said yes to him. It was in those six months that Mira got to know him better, well enough to choose him as her partner for life. She didn't care what her friends said about him, she was oblivious to everyone else's views, listening only to her heart. Her world had suddenly transformed. It had acquired a new colour – the colour of love, which is blinding for the two hearts involved. They think they perceive everything the same way as they did, before the advent of love but, little do they realise, that even though little seemed to have changed, something *had* changed indeed.

It was as if the streets remained the same, the cars honked the same way as before, the same people spat on the roads and threw garbage on the ground. It was the same old heat, the scalding sun and pollution clogging the streets and minds of Delhi and then, almost in a flash, Mira's eyes would rest on an elderly couple, trembling together and crossing the road with their hands clasped, and what she felt inside at that moment, made her realise how deep she was in the ocean of love. It was that feeling which made her take the long route back home, just so she could get twenty minutes extra with a person who could make them last for eternity.

These were the kind of feelings developing in them both. At least, these feelings developed right away in Mira. For Veer, the essence of love came much later, when they were three months into a relationship and their classes were on the verge of ending. There was an ominous uncertainty about the future and he was perturbed only by the fact that he wouldn't be seeing her every day. He was so overcome by this feeling that, on their last working day, he had planted a small peck on her cheek as she was leaving.

But the end of their coaching classes did not mean an end to their love, unlike many other couples, and they devised ways to meet each other. They came for regular tests, even after the classes had ended, not because they wanted to study, but because they wanted to see each other, even if it meant waking up at six in the morning and taking the seven thirty test.

When so much was happening in their personal lives, their supposed entrance exam preparation inevitably had to take a back seat. With the budding romance that was destined to last for a lifetime, each of them realised that they wanted something else in life, not to become a doctor. While Mira resumed her love of writing, Veer became engrossed in various managing vocations, such as event-management to get an idea of the kind of life he wanted.

That period was the hardest time of their first splendid year together, especially for her, as she had to break the news to her family, telling them that she wanted to drop medicine and pursue literature, because in her heart she had always aspired to be a writer.

It amused her, because the more she speculated on how tough it was going to be, the easier it actually was when she dared to speak her mind, especially to the head of the family. But her father was quite easily mellowed into accepting her decision, largely because he hoped to push her towards the civil services after graduation.

For Veer, things ran smoothly on the academic front. He decided on graduation followed by an MBA – his plan was a startup, but the ideas were too many and the wait was long for the implementation of those ideas.

Time changes for none and moves at its own free pace, but he did eventually get to live his dream of creating a start-up company, in the future, just as Mira got to publish a book.

It was around this time, when they both were at a crucial stage of deciding their careers, when another great milestone was achieved in their love story.

"I want to kiss you," Veer texted her one Sunday morning and Mira blushed on reading the message.

"All right, your wish shall be granted ;)" she texted him back, surprised at her own audacity to finally agree to fulfil his wish, which had been persistent for over a month. It wasn't that his requests made her uncomfortable since they both knew that she wanted

75

it too, but she had been apprehensive about the physical part of being in a relationship.

She remembered how, after she had expressed her love for Veer, after their six-month long courtship, he had made a physical contact with her the very next day. What he had done was not really a great deal, but its impact on Mira had been enormous. He had simply pushed a straying strand of hair behind her ears, without touching her skin at all. Technically, he had only touched the dead cells of her hair, but it seemed to her as though every cell of her being had come alive, carrying the impulse of his touch all the way to her heart, which was pumping blood at an exceptional rate. Her ears had grown hot, her breathing fast, and her skin pale. She would remember forever how vibrantly he had laughed at her, instantly easing her tension. Such was Mira, so pure and guileless in matters of love.

She believed that love stories that began at an early and crucial age tended to go far, because when we are just out of our teens, we share our thoughts, expressions and especially opinions with such an individual who is not only our friend but also partner for life and hence the psychic development of the two lovers is such that each gets amalgamated into the system of another, leading to a better understanding between them. Also, their influence over each other shapes them into better individuals and a loving couple, as happened in the case of Veer and Mira.

It was gradually that holding hands, occasional hugs and pecks on the cheeks became normal for them – and then, about after four to five months of being together, came their first kiss. First in both the literal and metaphorical sense.

In Mira's case, it was the literal sense because Veer was the first man she had come close to and, for him, the metaphorical sense because, though he had had one girlfriend in the past, he was purged of all emotions in his kiss with this one sublime woman.

She had lost control of her senses the moment his lips touched hers, while he had thought that she had lost consciousness. It was in that moment that he had gathered Mira in his arms, held her from falling apart, and had transferred new energy and life into her soul, the passion invigorating her to respond to his kiss.

It was in the same moment that she realised, for the first time, what it truly meant to be attracted to someone.

With one hand at her waist and with the other drawing away the long hair falling on her neck and shoulders, Veer had simply touched his lips to her neck in a gentle kiss. That small gesture had run like wildfire through her body, making her shiver in his arms. At that moment, Mira's thoughts were – chaos and jumble.

Veer's mind, however, was as focused and clear as crystal. There was only one thought in his mind, reverberating endlessly, which was – 'I want this woman to be mine, forever,' and not being the slow and steady kind, he had gone down on his knees to proclaim, "I love you!" looking up at her. She had been surprised, but very happy and she too had gone down on her knees and whispered the same in his ears. The interlocking-embrace that followed was worth remembering for both of them.

CHAPTER ELEVEN

Veer and Mira did not have the perfect relationship. But they were conscious of working on their relationship with each passing unit of time. They strived never to let go of one another, in spite of breaking up seven times in a year and a half, with each 'break up' lasting not more than twenty-four hours.

It was evident then that they had numerous disagreements and arguments and they fought over the most trivial of things.

"Why didn't you put henna on your hands this season?" Veer asked her one evening, irritation dripping from his voice. Mira had known that he loved seeing henna on her hands, but she hadn't realised that such a small issue would develop into a day-long tiff between them.

Mira's reasons for being angry with him were also not very substantial, in fact, they were bizarre. Once, she had had an argument with him over a glass of pineapple juice. He had been insisting that she should have a glass of juice at the mall, because she had fasted all day. She had found his persistence very annoying because she hadn't wanted to consume anything from outside, because she believed it would contain salt. Though what Veer had been saying was for her benefit, she had not budged from her stance and, again, this had been enough for a quarrel between them, lasting two whole days.

But deep in their hearts, both of them were content that they fought over trivial issues and each of them wished that they would rather continue these insignificant tiffs because, after making peace, their love for each other was more than doubled. Besides, they never wanted big problems to seep in between them.

In their relationship, loyalty being an issue was simply out of the question. It was understood on both sides that they would never have to doubt each other in matters concerning their fidelity. Even if a third person tried to enter, or break, their bond of love, their confidence in each other was enough to kick the intruder out.

Neither of them knew that their Fate was to be disloyal to them. The six years they spent together were exclusively about the two of them – their love, romance, passion and how they were the perfect couple in the eyes of their friends.

As the years passed, Mira realised what it was to fall in love with the same person over and over again. She realised what it was to be truly delighted without any reason, what it was to have your pain eased by sharing it with someone who would never be judgmental about what was unravelling in your head, one who would understand you, always. The bond of their love grew stronger and deeper as they got to know each other better and neither of them realised how deeply they had fallen into this bottomless pit of love, or noticed how willingly they had worked towards this fall.

Mira's relationship with Veer also had a balmy effect on her otherwise turbulent life, be it quarrels with her family members, especially her father, problems with friends or academics or other stresses at work, they all found a culminating point in him and he would guide her to work out solutions for herself.

This counselling, however, worked both ways as it was not that always Mira who needed his help. Many times, she played a good listener, mentored him to overcome hurdles in his life and gave him sound career advice. In a nutshell, they had each other's backs.

However, there were also days when they themselves were the reason of discord in their lives and to add to their misery, they had no one to turn to when they fought with one another. That was why, within a day or two, their hearts always compelled them to give in to each other. They fought, they cried, they kissed and, finally, they made up, either in bed or during their late night going-on-early morning phone calls.

Most of the time they fought on movie dates, on birthdays and it was only two of their anniversaries that escaped being fought over, but, they loved each other for all the remaining days of the year. In a way, perhaps they were better than those couples who expressed love only on special occasions, rather than every day.

From the very beginning, it was evident that their love was unlike other contemporary relationships.

They seemed destined to be together and, most importantly, they strived to be together. They had had numerous ups and downs in their six years together, but they had been able to surpass all of them just with the intention of truly wanting to be with each other.

CHAPTER TWELVE

Mira and Veer didn't get into the same college for graduation, even after trying very hard, but they were glad that they would still be in the same city. In order to meet every day, they had to make amendments to their normal routine and, therefore, both of them had to bunk occasional classes. There were times when they bunked college for an entire week to enjoy some time alone, just the two of them, and there were times they couldn't see each other for a whole week, because they had assignments and other work to commit to. Correction – Mira had other work to commit to. For Veer, there had been no priority over her, be it classes or anything else.

During the initial years of this set-up they had fought a lot, because he had always felt that they weren't spending enough time together, while she had felt that her classes, assignments, and presentations were more important, because they were in the career-making years of their lives.

The art of balancing their priorities was something

82

that came slowly to them, after numerous fights and endless tears.

In the beginning, Mira had often been very irritated at this immaturity on his part, because he wasn't as serious with his studies as she was. She wanted Veer to realise that everybody had various facets of their lives – that there could be a life other than one's love life.

Veer, on the other hand, ridiculed this idea of hers. For him, love was the only life and though he never told her, he was hurt by her way of thinking. Eventually, time proved him right, because, their love did, indeed, become the entirety of life for Mira, but only after their relationship had come to an end.

That there might be some truth to his idea of love being life had hit her before, maybe in the fourth year of their relationship, as Mira had gradually begun to focus more and more on him. Her social life reduced drastically and all of it boiled down to spending time with Veer. This change was not something she regretted. In fact, she was surprised at how happy she was to devote all her time to him. For them, as a couple, meeting options were restricted because of Mira's fixed curfew. She had to be home by six or six-thirty, at any cost, and she couldn't go away for outings by herself on weekends. Unlike other boys, who would complain at these limitations, he understood each and every one of them.

Both of them had many good friends. He brought them all together and, as a result, they had a large number of people for outings to movies or dances or lunches. Day trips were in abundance for both of their groups, as they thoroughly enjoyed their college lives by exploring every nook and corner of Delhi, be it the Book Fair and other fairs at the Pragati Maidan, the amusement parks like Worlds of Wonder, or Adventure Island, or heritage sites like Qutub Minar, Jantar Mantar, Jama Masjid, Red Fort, Old fort, and also the Delhi Zoo. The number of sight-seeing points in Delhi makes up a long list and this group of youngsters enjoyed their time by romancing and basking in the glory of these monuments.

It was in their final year at college that the friends planned an unofficial trip to Agra. Of course, this plan would have had no outcome, because the girls would never get permission for an unofficial overnight trip. Mira would certainly not get permission, even if she was on her deathbed. Her grumpy father had never allowed her on overnight trips, even while she was in an all girls' school, with female teachers as guardians, and here was a trip being planned by her friends, completely unofficial and one which included boys.

Who other than Veer could suggest a midway between the two extreme situations? He came up with a plan that was excellent, but also dangerous, and the only hurdle to executing it was convincing Mira.

"Guys," he began in his controlled, persuasive tone, "I have the perfect solution to this problem," a smirk already adorned his face, because his managing-mind had devised the perfect plan, and even if it wasn't that perfect, Veer knew how to convince his friends into believing that it was.

Needless to say, the others were excited at the prospect of a solution, but Mira sensed trouble ahead. She looked at him with eyes entreating him not to divulge his plan at all, because there was no way she was going to risk making a journey to Agra – outside of Delhi –without telling her parents. She knew that this was something even her mother would not give permission for.

Veer, however, chose to dismiss her warning looks. He could always dismiss her fears later because, for him, the priority was getting everybody to accept his plan and, all the more, he wasn't going to pay heed to her, because the idea of visiting the Taj Mahal with her was something he couldn't let go of - a chance to go visit the evergreen token of love with his love.

"See, it's very simple," he said, "Agra is a two and a half hour ride from Delhi, right?" his voice adopted a convincing attitude with which Mira was well acquainted.

"Right!" agreed the others in unison, some of them nodding their heads, their eyes dancing at the adventure that lay ahead, something that would, naturally, involve breaking the rules.

"Okay, then it's all sorted," said Veer, his hands resting on his back and a twisted smile on his face, because he knew that half the work was done and that Mira was getting restless and agitated.

She wanted him to shut up and not drive her into unnecessary dilemmas, but these thoughts remained in her head.

"We can all meet at the Kashmere Gate metro station at 8 a.m. sharp," he continued, "and then drive to Agra via the Yamuna Expressway." He paused, as if to evaluate the plan further in his head. "Don't worry about the car," he said. "That's my job and, thereafter, we can share the drive."

After another moment of calculation, he resumed, "we can reach the city by 10.30 a.m. latest by 11 a.m."

As Veer spoke, everyone listened with their eyes and ears glued to him.

"We can visit Taj Mahal for say, 11 to 12, 12 to 1, 1 to 2, 2 to 3!" He began counting the time on his fingers to make four hours sound like one hour of sixty minutes and three-sixty seconds multiplied by four.

Such a manipulator he was, thought Mira, trying to avoid a smile.

"And then," he continued, "we can return by 3 p.m. and reach Delhi by 5.30 p.m. so that everybody can be home by 6.30 p.m. maximum."

Veer ended the sentence with his gaze fixed upon Mira, as if first seeking an answer from her. She was well versed with his tactics and she knew that he would eventually convince her to come along. She didn't want to miss this chance of seeing the Taj Mahal with him, but then, she could not take such a risk - if her father were to know, surely she wouldn't be alive much longer.

"I don't know! Don't look at me like that!" she said, shifting her eyes away from Veer, her face contorted into a doleful expression.

This time he did not need to persuade her further, because their friends were more than willing to do the task. He wanted her to subdue the baseless inhibitions she festered in her mind. He wanted her to learn from her own decisions and enjoy life the way she wanted to, not the way someone else dictated her to.

"No, no, Mira, we are not hearing anything against this now," one of their female friends blurted out. "You know this plan suits us. I mean, it's tailor made for us. There won't be any risk. Please Mira, say yes!"

One by one, each of them started pleading, because they knew that if she refused to come, the plan would be cancelled, as Veer wouldn't want to come and there wouldn't be any car without him.

"Please Mira, please say yes!" said one voice.

"Mira, please do it for us. It is the last year of college, and think of it, so much fun. Let us make some memories to hold on to," said another voice.

"But what if something goes wrong?" Mira questioned, "what if our car broke down or what if, what if we were to have an accident?" She began to list out every possible reason for this trip being a bad idea.

Veer saw through her reluctance and realised that this was asking too much from her. She was having a hard time deciding and her eyes bore the expression of being entangled in an unwanted mess. He took her by the hand, snatching her away from the crowd and leading her aside, "Come with me," was all he said.

The others sat back and enjoyed the meal they were having at the food court in a mall, content and excited about the prospective trip. Veer knew how to prompt Mira, dispel her fears and make her step into the shoes of her life and believe in her decisions, to help her live free from restraints.

"Love, you know that such a chance to visit the Taj Mahal together may never come back to us," he said, cupping her face in his hands and looking intently at her face. "I promise nothing will go wrong. I promise you won't regret it."

Mira kept debating whether to give in or not. Of course, she wanted to go with him on this romantic journey, but too much was at stake. Still, the captivation of a chance of being with Veer from morning to evening at the place of love – the Taj Mahal – was already taking hold of her.

"Just trust me for one day," he said, rubbing his thumb across her cheeks down to her lips.

She looked down and then up again at his face, into his eyes and she thought, 'This is want I want.' She smiled at him. "Okay!" she said, hugging him tight.

After a short embrace, he whispered in her ears, "You had better run away from me, or I'll kiss you right here and now." Veer's eyes were playful as she ran away from him shouting, "Now, you'll get your treat at the Taj Mahal!" She winked at him from a distance.

Veer stood blushing as he thought of how beautiful she looked, once the clouds of doubt had been dodged away from her mind.

CHAPTER THIRTEEN

Once everything was prepared, all that remained was for the trip to Agra to actually take place.

Mira had been ecstatic and she had wanted the day to stop for some time, so that this short trip may extend into eternity. She had chosen a wrap around blue printed skirt, ankle length, and had teamed a plain white top with it. She thought that this would be both casual and comfortable, and would also ease the summer heat. She wore plain studded diamonds in her ears, pulled her hair back into a casual ponytail and opted for matching *kolhapuri chappals*. A pretty scarf, draped around her neck in unequal knot, added glamour to the look.

Pleased with what she saw in the mirror as a reflection of herself, Mira picked up her handbag, containing every item she could possibly need, including a first aid box, a portable charger and sanitary napkins, and stepped out of the house.

She started at 7.30 a.m. in the morning, and sneaked out before her father woke up and objected to any invisible indecencies in her outfit. She had cooked up a story for her mother, as to why she would be late that day, saying that they were going on an official day trip to some exotic farm on the outskirts of Delhi, which involved a trek and other activities.

Mira knew she wasn't exactly dressed for a trek, but her mother usually chose to ignore her clothing, as long as her daughter looked happy. Mira was careful not to make up any further explanations, fearing a slip of the tongue. She was already upset about having to lie to her mother.

The meeting point had been decided as the Kashmere Gate metro station, because that was close to the Yamuna Expressway and convenient for everyone to reach within the stipulated time. Out of eight people, six were already there, while two of them took their own sweet time to come.

It was after a wait of twenty minutes that they arrived with a huge bag, which clinked with beer bottles. Of course, Kanchan and Rajat could not have left without the most important guests of the trip – alcohol and cigarettes. They had three bottles of beer and a few packs of smokes, as more than that would have meant danger, besides Rajat was supposed to be driving.

There were four, in the group, who consumed alcohol and three who smoked. These were common pitfalls of studying in Delhi University, but Mira and Veer had avoided such traps. Of course, they believed that everybody had a right to exercise their own choices, but, moderation was the key to leading a balanced life and moderation was something that each of them knew, except Kanchan, who had to be checked constantly, because she had a tendency to overdo things.

However, they had no fear of Kanchan losing control today, due to the scanty resources they had permitted on-board, just enough to lighten their spirits. It was decided that Rajat was to drive first, and Mira would get to spend time in the back seat with her beloved.

As soon as they had settled in the car and begun their journey, Veer sat back, relaxed. His left arm lay on the back rest of the seat as he motioned Mira, with his eyes, to sit close to him, and rest her head on his arm. Mira had to agree. Why would she want to miss a chance like this? He entangled his fingers in her hair, like he always did when her head rested against his arm and they were all set for a beautiful day.

The car radio was tuned to the melodious voice of some unknown singer, who sang remixed versions of classic songs. It had to be. With Rajat on the roll, one could expect no less than an acoustic version of 'Kabhi kabhi mere dil mein khyaal aata hai' with everybody singing at the top of their voices.

"Did I tell you how ravishing you look today," Mira whispered, awed by how well Veer was dressed, in a simple blue and white check shirt, blue trousers and his homely Crocs. He smiled at her and his eyes lit up at the sudden compliment, something which he should have made to her.

"You're no less!" he said, his eyes dancing to the melody of love, as he leaned in to plant a kiss on her neck, his hand moving from her shoulders down to the back of her waist, his fingers playing across her skin. She struggled to release herself from his hold.

"Behave," she said, as she shot an angry look at him, trying to retain the poker expression. He held the pointed finger and put it to his ear, "Scratch them for me, please," he said smiling. After a moment, they both burst out laughing, leaving everyone else puzzled.

Mira took out a box of chocolate cake she had made and brought with her, and everyone enjoyed eating it. The song on the stereo, changed to a soothing version of *'Baahon ke darmiyaan'* and got all the couples busy romancing. While Kanchan and Rajat sat in the front, singing the lyrics, or rather, screaming them at the top of their voices.

Everyone knew Kanchan and Rajat had a thing for each other, but they had never confessed their attraction and everyone was secretly hopeful that the trip would bring out their emotions towards each other. After all, a trip to the Taj Mahal should have some benefits for young lovers.

After finishing an entire chocolate cake, two packets of wafer chips, one helping of vegetable sandwiches and a can of apple juice, each of them was full and, of course, sleepy. In one and a half hours of driving, all of them had had enough chit chat, song, and even dance, after which, they all seemed to have fallen asleep, except Rajat, of course, because he was driving. Kanchan and Mira, too, were awake.

Mira couldn't sleep because she didn't want to miss even a moment of their journey, and Veer was sleeping with his head in her lap, so she sat stroking his hair, studying his innocent face, and also kissing him occasionally – softly, without waking him up. She knew he had not slept until very late the previous night and had also had to wake up early. He had been so engaged in arranging the car, license and other papers that were needed to take a car outstation. Moreover, it was his cousin's car, so all the papers for this group of youngsters were needed, in case they were faced with a problem.

No matter how free spirited and fun loving he seemed, she knew that Veer was worried about getting his friends, especially Mira, and the car safely back to Delhi. She had been his top most priority, because she had trusted him, and only him, in agreeing to this adventure.

She kept stroking his hair, thinking about his ardent love for her. While on this trip, she felt as if they were on their honeymoon. It was no less than a dream come true, and she realised how blindly she trusted Veer and how secure she felt with him, so many kilometres away from home and family. She realised that this person sleeping with his head in her lap was also her family, a family that she had chosen for herself.

Mira planted a quick kiss on his cheeks, disrupting his sleep and making him look up at her with twinkling sleepy eyes and murmur, "Mmm... Please let me sleep love," as a smile spread across his lips. He kissed her stomach since he slept facing it, closed his eyes, took her hand and put it back on his head. Then he went straight back into his slumber.

Meanwhile, Rajat was having a hard time staying awake, he yawned a couple of times, shook his head vigorously, to snap out of sleepiness, and stopped the car. He looked around, first on the road and then at his friends and Kanchan.

"Ugh!" Rajat muttered to himself, when he found everyone sleeping, while he had to drive. As he turned back to face the road and start driving again, he found Kanchan missing from the seat beside him. He looked about, frantically searching for his friend, who had jumped out of the car all of a sudden. He spotted her standing beside the road, facing vast stretches of land. He observed her for a while, wondering what was she up to.

"When did she jump out of the car?" he said to himself, and got out of the car with a bottle of beer in his hand.

Mira, who had been awake all this time, was wondering why Rajat had stopped the car and what was Kanchan doing outside. Just as she was about to ask him, he stepped out of the car and banged the door shut.

A new idea sprung up in Mira's mind and she smiled, wondering whether this could be the start of a new love story – between two of her friends. Could they make it happen? 'No, I'm just over thinking as usual,' she checked herself and continued watching them through the window.

She saw that Rajat now stood besides Kanchan and it seemed as if they were engaged in a deep discussion of some kind. 'Kanchan must be musing over her theories inspired from nature again' thought Mira, but that was just a wild guess. In reality, she had no clue what Kanchan and Rajat were discussing, even though she wanted to know.

Rajat walked up to Kanchan with a sealed bottle of beer in his hand. "Is this is what you want?" he said, offering her the bottle.

She looked at him as if she was waiting for him to come to her. "No." she replied.

They remained silent for a while.

"You know, we should get going, Kanchan." Rajat began, trying not to look straight into her eyes, "if they see us here together, the teasing will start all over again."

Kanchan smiled at him, a meek smile, "To think of it," she said, "I like it when they tease us!" looking directly at him.

Rajat was astounded. He had planned to express his love for her when they were at the Taj Mahal, but he had still been debating inside, unable to figure out her feelings and, here she stood, dropping hints at him and snatching the words away from his mouth. They looked at each other intently, for a while, until Kanchan broke her gaze away, blushing and a little annoyed at him for not taking the first step. Rajat's heart was pounding. He was staring at her and, in the next moment, he took her hand and pulled her closer to him. He kissed Kanchan, a fully fledged lip lock, something they both found hard to draw away from.

'My, my!' thought Mira, delighted to witness this wild moment of passion between her friends. A smile broke across her face and she woke up Veer urgently.

"Wake up, love, you're missing something," as she

shook him.

As he woke up and rubbed his eyes, he couldn't help laughing at what he saw.

"Kanchan and Rajat!" he exclaimed, looking first at them and then at Mira. "Okay, okay, enough, get a room guys," he whispered cheerfully, as Mira laughed at the little secret love they had witnessed.

They saw Rajat and Kanchan break away, smiling at each other, both looking happy and satisfied. As they returned to the car, Veer positioned himself back in Mira's lap.

"Love, act like you're sleeping," he said, shutting his eyes tight. Mira too, rested her head against the window as if she were asleep.

"I don't think anybody saw us," said Kanchan, when they got back to the car. She looked relieved.

"No, we didn't!" blurted the couple from the back seat, sitting up to face the brand new lovers. Naturally, they hadn't been able to keep themselves from admitting that they knew about the love story cooking between their friends. And the looks on Kanchan and Rajat's faces were too valuable to miss.

"Don't worry!" said Mira, "just pretend we never said anything and enjoy your ride."

"I'm going to kill you if you open your mouths!" exclaimed Rajat, blushing, as he put the keys back in the ignition and started the car.

CHAPTER FOURTEEN

The Taj Mahal required a ticket of twenty rupees per person, a relatively cheap price for visiting one of the Seven Wonders of the World.

All of them moved, in a group, towards the big entrance gate, sifting through various security checkpoints which prevented people from carrying eatables or beverages into the monument.

The entrance to the Taj Mahal had a beautiful archaic gate. Mira thought it would be improper to call it a door. Seen from there, the marble monument appeared as a symmetrical mass of beauty. The white – well, a tad-bit yellow, actually – mesmerizing dome and pillars, constructed on a large elevated platform, reflected the beauty of Taj as a sculpture made by God and left on Earth, for mankind to perish in its beauty.

That supreme token of love induced feelings of awe and wonder, especially in those who saw it for the first time.

Mira had been to the Taj Mahal twice in her life but, that day, when she saw it – her hand tightly clasped in Veer's – she understood the true nuances of love associated with that eternal structure.

Standing at the huge entrance, each of them had their own experience of witnessing the stark beauty of the Taj Mahal against the backdrop of an industrial town of Agra. It was the smoke, litter and filth of this industrial town that was slowly jaundicing at the beautiful Taj, turning it yellow, over time. Still the trance that its beauty created was in no way diminished.

Even though it was a weekday, the rush was unimaginable. From freshly married couples flocking to Agra for a romantic honeymoon, to the huge number of foreigners visiting the seventh wonder of the world and getting their photographs, especially the girls, taking photos with the indigenous people of India, ensuring a surge of likes and comments on their Facebook profile pictures of those Indian tourists. Amidst the chaos and rush, the overall experience were breathtaking.

As soon as their group entered the gate, there lay a stretch of fountains and greenery and, also, a square shaped platform, ridden with people at every step, trying to get photographs of themselves holding the tip of Taj Mahal's dome. That is how the local photography business flourished in Agra, by alluring over excited Indians into getting such weird photographs taken.

Mira looked around at her friends, each of them was doing their own thing – the eight people had split into smaller groups to explore every nuance and facet of the great monument. The only instruction was to return to the main door, unfailingly, by 3.00 p.m., leaving them with three and a half hours to roam about.

When she was left alone with Veer, to enjoy this 'practice honeymoon' as she had chosen to term it, she realised that he hadn't spoken a word since laying his eyes on the Taj Mahal.

"Hey," she nudged him, "say something!"

Veer turned his eyes from the white structure to look at Mira. "Do you also feel it?" he asked.

Mira looked into his eyes, puzzled and unsure of what he was referring to.

"Do you also feel a special connection with this place?" he continued.

Mira nodded in agreement. She could see the amazement in his eyes and she concluded that he had lost his mind because of the unsettling beauty of the monument that stood ahead of them, at a distance of only a few feet.

"Yes," she answered him. "And do you feel as if you're looking at this place through the eyes of Shah Jahan?" she continued, playfully.

Veer stared at her in mock disbelief, "How could you possibly know?"

"Because I feel like Nur Jahan myself!" she laughed, with a light punch to his arm.

He laughed and put his arms around her, pulling her closer, so that her head rested on his arm, near the shoulders, as they stood devouring the majesty of what stood in front of them, the most magnificent creation of mankind. They didn't need any words to describe what they felt. Their eyes bore enough witness to the emotional rush inside them. What they felt inside was exactly what every other couple in love felt when they saw this epitome of love. They felt their love to be inscribed in the history of the Taj Mahal, in the history that harboured Shah Jahan's love for his wife, Nur Jahan. Time seemed to have stopped as they stood facing such perfection and wondering if their love would stand out among the rest, as being so pious and ethereal.

"Come, let's go inside!" said Mira, pulling Veer by the arm, "you must see the intricate carvings on the interior walls, and you have to experience the smell."

"What smell?" he asked, wondering what could go wrong in the perfection of the beauteous structure.

"Well," replied Mira, "when you go inside to visit the tomb of Nur Jahan, you get this peculiar smell of the dead." She wrinkled her tiny nose, remembering her previous visits. "The last time, *Maa* and I couldn't even enter the tomb area, it was so flushed with the odour of all those living human beings, plus the dead."

"Mira," he began, feigning unhappiness. "No spoilers! Don't try and steal my first experience from me."

"All right, I won't say a word now," she replied, smiling.

They reached the platform on which the monument was erected. A steep, narrow staircase led upwards, to the dome, but first, they had to change into clean white galoshes as shoes were not allowed on the white marble, lest the dirt should stick to it.

The Taj Mahal had been created keeping perfect symmetry in mind and it looked the same when

100

viewed from any direction. The towers and tombs were carved with illusory designs and gave the impression of widening at the top, when viewed from the base. The walls were engraved with colourful paintings and red and green flower structures. There were also empty sockets, which were said to have once contained rubies and diamonds and many other precious stones, before they were looted by the British Empire, and others who had ruled over India for a considerable time, long enough to deplete the country of its resources.

Veer and Mira moved forward, along with the queue of people who encircled the dome, visiting each side of it and also, inside it, in a circle.

At the back of the main structure, river Yamuna streamed in its most serene form, giving an overall calming effect to the buzzing industrial town of Agra. Together, they explored every inch of the Taj Mahal, not just inspecting with their eyes, but also feeling the cold white marble against their hands and, of course, their noses had also started working by the time they entered the tomb area.

"You were right about the smell," said Veer, his voice squeaky because he had pinched his nose and covered his mouth with his hands. Mira gave him an 'I-told-you-so' look and pulled him away from the tomb area and into the open, for some fresh air.

"Ah!" she gasped, gulping in bouts of fresh air, which yet seemed tainted with dust.

"What is the point of visiting the tomb anyway?" exclaimed Veer, "I mean, why disturb the dead with your queer eyes?"

Veer laughed and Mira nudged him with a reprimanding look on her face. "Respect okay?" she said as he put his hands up in surrender, still laughing. He suddenly turned towards her and looked straight into her eyes, reaching out for her hand to hold it.

"Romeo mode on!" she laughed as she playfully pressed his nose with her finger. "And that's your turn-on-button," she chuckled.

He gave a slight laugh, his eyes sparkling with love for her, "Thank you," he said planting a small kiss on her cheek. She rubbed the place where Veer had kissed her with her fingers and looked around to make sure that nobody had seen them. India still functioned on moral policing but, of course, he didn't care about anything besides them. He was overwhelmed because the woman he loved was standing in front of him and he could see the same love he felt, reflected in her eyes.

"Thank you for making my first visit to the Taj Mahal so special," he said, happiness radiating from his face, "and, most importantly, thank you for trusting me. I know this trip was asking a lot from you." He looked at her intently and his expression changed from jovial to serene.

Mira was more than happy to be here with him. In her heart, she thanked god for making her so lucky in matters of love. She had never dreamt of a man like this in her life, yet this was more than a dream come true – it was like living with her dream.

"You can make up for it next time we meet," she teased him, her eyes dancing.

A broad smile broke across his face. "So, will it be your place or mine?" he asked.

Mira rolled her eyes, laughing at his theatrics. "When has it ever been mine?" she chortled.

"Someday," replied Veer, with his fingers crossed and his hands on either side of her neck, resting on her shoulders.

She pulled herself away and dragged him along, "come, we must find the others. A group photograph is mandatory."

"No," he interjected. "Not yet. First, I want to spend some time alone with you!" He took her by the arm, leading her down the steps and towards the surrounding gardens. She followed him happily, willing to go anywhere he wanted to take her.

They stopped next to a tree, actually, many trees and a handful of tourists. Veer made her sit on an empty bench and looked around, as if wishing the other people to go away.

She looked carefully at him, confused, "Love, I hope you aren't thinking of getting mushy here," she said, getting up at once, as if wanting to go, but he held her hand and made her sit down again.

"Can't you sit still for some time?" he said, his eyes directed at her. His voice seemed nervous.

After more looking around for some time more, when Veer was sure that no one was looking, he knelt in front of her and held her hands. A blush crept across his face, making him look very charming and his smile was so radiant that it reached up to his eyes to light them. Slowly, he gathered courage, but when he

103

looked up and saw her trying to hide a naughty smile, he too broke into laughter.

"Don't look at me like that," he entreated, burying his face in his hands, "it isn't easy, Mira!" Veer regained his composure and Mira gave him a supportive smile and waited patiently. "Mira," he said, "my love-"

His phone started ringing.

"Oh, damn!" he swore, taking the phone out of his pocket. He saw 'Maa' flashing across the screen. He made a begging face at her and she nodded, allowing him to take the call. "Yes Maa," he said.

She waited patiently. She was still very excited to know what Veer was planning to say to her that had made him so nervous. At that point, she received a text message from Kanchan. "Where are you both? Come to the main area ASAP!"

Mira began to worry, her mind over-thinking, overworking and conjecturing what could have happened. Was there an emergency? Since she did not have enough balance to make a roaming call from her number, she waited for Veer to finish speaking to his mother, motioning him to hurry up, whenever he glanced in her direction.

After what seemed like eternity, he came up to her, explaining how his elder brother had leaked news of his Agra trip to their mother and that she had been aghast at the thought of her son being alone on an outstation trip. It had taken him ten minutes to explain to her that he was not alone, that he had seven other friends along with him and that everything was all right.

As he walked towards Mira, smiling and pinching one of his ears with his fingers, gesturing an apology, she held him by the hand and began to walk away from that spot, "Kanchan texted. She wants us there ASAP. I think there is some emergency," she blurted, leading him away.

Veer stopped abruptly and pulled her hard towards himself, so hard that she landed glued to his body. He wrapped his arms around her, pulling her even closer to himself. She blushed, all at once, her nose a special shade of red as she stood wrapped in his arms with his face so close to hers that she could feel his warm breath on her hair.

"This is an even graver emergency," he murmured, his voice hoarse and sexy as he blew a strand of hair away from her face.

"You had better stop all this," she said, softly reprimanding him in a voice that hardly escaped her lips, as faint as her breath. She was enjoying the moment, but was also afraid, lest some policeman saw them in such an 'objectionable' position. As she struggled to release herself from his hold, Veer tightened his arms around her and held her right hand behind her waist, almost twisting it, but lightly, playfully.

"I will not let you go," he asserted, looking directly in her eyes. "Ever."

"But not here, love," she protested, "please understand!"

Veer shushed her and took her left hand in his. He opened her palm and slipped a silver coloured ring onto her ring finger.

105

Mira was overwhelmed, she was out of her senses, and she looked at him intently. There were no tears in her eyes, only love – love for the man who stood in front of her. She kissed him on the nose, unable to decide how to react because the magic and romance of the moment was too much to handle.

Veer let go of her and smiled, holding her left hand and lifting it up to his lips to kiss it. "I am not going to ask you to be mine forever, Mira, I'm going to make sure you are mine forever and, for that, I promise to be at your service for the rest of my life, my love."

As he finished uttering these magical words, Mira hugged him, hard. As they embraced, a soft breeze began to blow and yellow flowers came swirling past them, almost as a shower of tiny florets. When Mira opened her eyes and found them amidst the shower, her heart leapt with joy, because she believed that Nature had given their union its blessing.

"And there is no emergency, Kanchan is calling everyone for photographs," he said, laughing, without breaking the embrace. Mira smiled with her head rested against his chest. She needed nothing else from the universe because he was the most perfect gift.

*

Indeed, Kanchan had been calling everyone for photographs and the friends spent the last hour of the delightful trip taking pictures of themselves and each other – solo pictures, couples pictures and group photographs of all genres could be found.

It was almost 3:00 p.m. by the time they began to

move out of the monument. They had decided upon a late afternoon lunch at some *dhaba* on the Yamuna Expressway, while returning to Delhi. This time, the driving duty rested on Veer and she sat next to him, while the others settled back into the car in more or less the same position as before. The ride back home was a smooth one.

Veer drove really well and Mira kept him pepped up with her incessant talking, smiling, blushing and even singing. He kept glancing sideways at her. He wanted her to be by his side forever, sharing this seat forever and he kissed her ringed finger many times throughout the journey.

After a meal of *Dal makhani, Butter naan* and *Shahi paneer,* followed by beer and *lassi*, each to their liking, the group took to quiet gossiping and romancing till they reached Delhi around 6.30 p.m.

Veer dropped everybody else at the Kashmere Gate station, but Mira got a ride almost all the way home, as he dropped her at the metro station nearest to her house.

Before leaving, Mira quickly planted a sweet kiss on his lips and jumped out of the car, leaving him blushing to himself.

CHAPTER FIFTEEN

It was in the fifth year of their relationship, when Mira was four and twenty winters down and done with her post graduation, that Veer had come face to face with the idea of losing her.

She had been returning home from a job interview at Satyavati College, for the post of assistant professor on an ad hoc basis. She had not been very excited about this college, because it was an off campus, and not so famous, and she would have had problems commuting daily to Ashok Vihar. But she still went ahead with the interview, because this was her first offer and not many postgraduates got a chance to teach in the huge race for the lectureship. Luckily, her resume had not been rejected, unlike many others she knew and she had been called for the interview.

Meanwhile, Veer was posted in Pune for a six month provisional period with the company he had been placed with, prior to the completion of his MBA in International Business.

They had both wanted to start earning, as soon as possible, because they wanted to save some money together and, maybe, buy a house of their own. They were ardent to take their first step towards a secure future together. However, Mira had to go through an ordeal before that which involved nothing less than facing death. This coming test had been uncalled for and she never saw it coming.

Mira left the metro station and began her walk home. It was her usual routine, and she had to cross two roads and one check point before, eventually, walking towards her residential area. The entire route was only a fifteen minute walk and Mira hated wasting ten rupees on an electric rickshaw, especially for such a short distance. There were times when she did, but only when she was not feeling well, or when she had worn high heels to work or college.

She talked to Veer on the phone as she walked, filling him in with the details of the interview, and explaining how she had been hoping for a better college to call her. She asked him about his training programme and, of course, whether he had eaten lunch or not – the most important topic in their everyday conversation. Somehow, Mira was always concerned about his food habits, as Delhi had been much of a struggle for him because he lived as a paying guest and then in a hostel which served pathetic food. She kept forgetting that in Pune, Veer stayed with his brother, and his sister in law was a sweet lady who took care of him.

After being assured that he had had some lunch, which his *bhabhi* had packed for him, they said goodbye and Mira put her cell phone back in her purse. She walked for about a hundred meters on the footpath and then turned left onto a divided road, crossing which she reached the main road. This road was quite dangerous because the red light at the check point worked erratically at times. There had been many mishaps on this particular road, so Mira had always been extra careful while on it. She had a good habit of crossing the road only at the red light, or with a group of other pedestrians, and she always taught others to do the same.

As she crossed that two-lane main road, she took a left and started walking towards her residential area. This time she just had to cross one road and enter the gate to her colony. She turned her head to look for any possible vehicles, but there weren't any, so she began to cross the road. Midway, again, she turned to see if any vehicles were coming, but still, she saw none.

It was as Mira reached the edge of the road and relaxed, that she suddenly felt a huge thud hitting her from the left. She was thrown uncontrollably into the middle of the road, where she lay lifeless. Her eyes were hazed and she could feel the hot blood gushing from the back of her head, but she had no strength to lift it. She thought that maybe her arm hurt and slowly she drifted towards numbness. She lay with her head resting on the ground, the dust filling her nose as she heaved. She could see cars stopping and hear the cries of the people gathering around her, but everything was misty and the sounds were muffled. She closed her eyes for a split second, to let reality seep in, but her head was throbbing too much, her heartbeat, produced an unusual warmth in her stomach that seemed to extend up to her throat. She opened her eyes and saw a man coming towards her, but she could hardly make out his face.

'It's him,' she thought, and that was the last thought she had.

*

It was 5.30 p.m. in the evening and Mira's mother was sitting in her office, growing restless, because she had been trying to call her daughter incessantly, but the call just wouldn't connect. It said the phone was either switched off or out of the coverage area.

"Where is this girl?!" she muttered angrily to herself. She was somewhat distracted for a while because a patient arrived, complaining of a high fever and running nose, so the next ten minutes were spent interrogating him about his symptoms and prescribing medicines. Her mind, however, kept returning to her daughter and wondering where she was. Mira hardly ever did this. Her phone was always sufficiently charged, so why would it just switch off like that? The mother checked herself. "No, I must not over think," she told herself, but, for some reason, the uneasiness didn't leave.

"Just take these medicines, for three days, and come back here if you don't feel better," she said to the patient, handing him the prescription.

Mira's mother was a doctor by profession, and she had a simple job, not the buzzing and pager-ing life of a private hospital, but the quiet life of a government CGHS dispensary, with a regular 10-6 job, usually at the desk. There were hardly any emergency calls.

At 5.30 p.m. her phone rang and she jumped to receive the call, thinking it must be from her daughter. Indeed it was, and she was relieved to see Mira's name on the screen of her phone. She prepared herself to reprimand her daughter for switching her phone off for so long, without

111

informing her about it.

"Hello Mira? Where are you?" she took off, in the high pitched tone that usually escaped her lips when she was stressed. She could hear a lot of noise from the other side, and sirens, either an ambulance or the police. Her heartbeat quickened. "Hello? Hello?" she shouted into the phone.

A man's voice replied. "Hello madam *ji*," he said, in a heavy Haryanvi accent. Mira's mother froze."Hello, Hello madam *ji*?" he continued. She gathered some strength to reply, her heart, confirming that something was definitely wrong.

"Yes?" Her voice quivered once and then, gaining control over herself, she said, "yes, this is my daughter's number you're calling from. Who am I speaking to?"

"There has been an accident, madam *ji*," he said, his voice loud and clear, ringing in her head. "We found this phone in a bag, next to the body, and other documents. Is your daughter's name Mira?"

'Accident' Mira's mother thought. "Body," she whispered, shaking uncontrollably. She sat down on the chair and tried to get hold of herself, but it was impossible.

The man on the phone kept repeating, "Hello, hello?" but the woman this side had no strength to reply. She was essentially weak at heart, especially regarding her family, 'Is she dead?' her mind wandered. 'No, it can't be,' her heart kept assuring her. But her mind kept repeating the word 'body' again and again.

The man hung up the phone, frustrated at a lack of response.

At that moment, her nurse entered the cabin and was aghast to see the doctor in such a state. There were tears in her eyes and darkness spread over her face.

"Doctor, Doctor Reena?" she shook Mira's mother, panicking.

"Mira," she whispered, looking up at the nurse with tear-filled eyes.

The nurse knew something terrible had happened because the look on the doctor's face gave everything away. She took the phone from the doctor's hand and dialled back the last received call, which was Mira's number.

After a frustrating amount of ringing, a man answered. "Hello!" he said, his voice reverberating in the background.

"Yes, hello?" the nurse replied. "What has happened to Mira? Is she okay?"

"Madam *ji*, there has been an accident. This girl was hit by a DTC bus," he replied, in a matter of fact tone.

The nurse grasped Dr. Reena's arm as she heard the news. "Is she okay?" she asked again, her voice shaky this time.

"Madam *ji*" she has been sent to the hospital, but we can't say anything about her condition. She has been taken to the L. B. Kapoor hospital, for now," said the bearer of unfortunate news, trying to sound as calm

113

as possible.

"Thank you," the nurse replied, hanging up on the call. She looked down at Dr. Reena. "Ma'am, we have to go," she said, shaking the mother out of her misery, there were tears welling in her eyes. "Mira is okay," she lied. "She needs you." Getting to the hospital was the priority, the mother could grieve later.

Dr. Reena looked up at her with hopeful eyes, "Is she really okay?"

The nurse nodded and took her by the arm to the wash basin. She told her to wash her face and relax, while she called a cab.

Dr. Reena settled a little, yet she was impatient to reach her daughter as quickly as she could. Then, she stopped, picked up her phone and dialled her husband's number, forgetting that she was upset with him because he had been harrowing Mira to sit for the civil service exams for the past few days, especially now that she was done with her post graduation. The call rang the full length and disconnected. She dialled again. This time Mira's father picked up the call at the very first ring.

"Yes," he answered, his voice relaxed, assuming that his wife had called to remind him of the *jalebis* he had to bring in the evening, in celebration of Mira's job interview.

"Mira," she had barely spoken when her voice broke.

"What happened to Mira?" he shouted from the other end, his heart rate rising quickly, but he could only hear his wife's sobs. "Reena, Reena!" he entreated.

114

"Please tell me what happened?" His voice was suddenly soft and measured.

"Mira had an accident. She's in LBK. Please come," she sobbed, speaking all at once.

"What?" he whispered, taken by shock, but suddenly he revived his spirits, "Reena, nothing will happen to our daughter," he said, knowing that she needed his support, "you go to her as fast as you can, I'll come at once."

She nodded at the phone, feeling a little better, now that her husband would take control of everything.

"And don't worry," he said, "I'll tell the other two that you're with me and we had to go somewhere."

He was secretly praying to God to keep his daughter safe. He had no idea what had happened, how the accident had occurred, but he kept praying.

It often happens, in times of strife, that our minds acquire this ability, the ability to hold on to faith, constantly. All the ego clashes and intellectual wars with his daughter were at bay. His daughter's life was most precious to him. After all, he loved her bitterly.

Even though Mira's mother and father were not usually compatible as a couple, there were times like these, when their love outshone the others. They worked like a machine in times of need, no matter how dysfunctional they were otherwise. For now, they seemed to comprehend each other's thoughts and actions completely.

God had found a way to unite this family once again, with love. But would this reunion be achieved at the cost of one of a life?

*

Mira had been in the ICU, with her eyes perpetually closed, for the past twenty hours. Her head was bandaged, there was a deep red scar under her eye, and her left arm lay folded on top of her.

Her face bore the expression of the dead. The room was full of medical instruments that beeped and pinged at every fragile beat of her heart. Her arms were punctured in numerous places, for the needles to administer medicines into her body. The only sign of life was the misting of the oxygen mask that covered her nose and the subsequent heaving of her bosom. Otherwise, she lay as still as stone and as pale as the moon.

Mira's family stood outside the room, watching through the glass door and crying, cursing, and praying for God to spare the life of their daughter. It had been twelve hours since the accident, but Mira had not yet regained consciousness, a sign of danger. This danger was evident from the looks on the faces of her doctors and, also her mother who, being a doctor herself, knew what the complications were. They said that if the patient didn't gain consciousness in the next twenty-four hours, she wouldn't be saved from slipping into a coma.

Her family prayed together for her. Her father was constantly consoling her mother, who broke down every time the nurse reported a "No response" from the patient.

"Please Reena, you have to hold on to yourself for Mira. She'll be all right, I know," he said to her, his voice cracking towards the end.

He left her there and rushed to hide his face, he couldn't weaken in front of his family, but he felt so helpless and the tears wouldn't stop rolling down his face. His mind kept repeating images of the times he had made his daughter cry, the times he had shouted at her, maybe even hit her, and he prayed to God, suddenly ashamed of himself.

"Please God, I never meant any of the things I said to her," he begged to the Almighty. "Please, save my child. I never told her, but I love her a lot."

He felt a hand on his shoulder and turned around to find his son, Aditya standing behind him, there were tears in his eyes, but more than tears of love, they were tears of sympathy towards his father, who he knew had been repenting relentlessly since seeing Mira on the hospital bed. At once, Mira's father hugged his son, who was already taller than him, at the age of eighteen, and the son wrapped his arms around the father and consoled him. There were tears streaming down his own eyes, as he silently wished the calamity to end soon.

"Papa," he said very softly to his father, who had been reduced to sobs in his arms. "Papa, please, you have to be the strength for all of us. You must not lose hope. Papa, you have to control mummy's grief. She's losing hope and she hasn't eaten anything after what happened. Are you listening?" he raised his father's face to look at him.

His father nodded, slowly at first, his eyes fixed proudly upon his grown-up son. He ran his hand through Aditya's hair and smiled back feebly at him. "Yes, you're right!" he whispered, as he straightened

117

up and walked towards the washbasin to wash his face and gather his strength. He was an IAS officer and he must not be weak. He could get the world's best doctors for his daughter at one phone call, so he decided to put all in his efforts in doing this.

Mira's mother, meanwhile, sat glued to her seat outside the room, wiping away her tears as she saw her daughter struggling to breathe. She knew how much Mira hated hospitals and how she didn't want to be a doctor because she could never bring herself to cut, sew and pierce a fellow human being. She thought of how much Mira hated coming to hospitals, and the way she feared dying in a hospital, because such deaths were full of pain. She had always harboured a mild phobia of acquiring some fatal disease and slowly losing her life, during painful and merciless treatments, with tubes stuck in her mouth and nose, and syringes in her body.

'And here you are, my dove,' her mother thought, 'just not opening your eyes'. Fresh tears welled up in her own and, again, she wiped them away. "Wake up darling," she whispered, looking intently at her daughter through the mist of her tears.

Ananya, lovingly called Anu, came and sat down next to her mother. She could see how disturbed the elder lady was. "Mother," she said, barely able to speak herself. "Don't worry, I know Mira will be all right."

She had brought a packet of biscuits for her parents to eat, because they were both patients with diabetes, and hadn't had a morsel of food since the accident. She feared they might lose their health, and there was no option of resting, because Mira would need all their attention.

"*Maa*, please have some of these, you don't want to fall sick, right?" she pleaded with her eyes.

Reena picked one up and nibbled on it aimlessly.

"What do the doctors say?" Anu questioned.

"There is internal bleeding, Anu, in the head and lungs. The bus hit her hard, directly on the back of the head." Her mother motioned with her hand to the point where Mira had been hit and started sobbing. "Oh my child, how scared she must have been!" she sighed, wanting to ease out her daughter's pain.

"*Maa*, why isn't she coming back?" said Ananya, looking questioningly at her mother and breaking down towards the end of the sentence.

Reena hugged her daughter. "Anu, I don't know, I just don't know, the internal bleeding should have stopped by now, but the medicines are not working," she cried, "I just know that we must keep praying, enough to make God give us back our daughter." Both the daughter and mother buried themselves into a deep prayer for Mira.

Aditya and his father returned to them, more controlled and calm now.

"Reena," Mira's father began, addressing his wife as she looked up at him, "Let's go home. We will freshen up and get some rest. Anu and Aditya can stay here," he said, clasping her hand to take her away.

"But," she resisted, reluctant to leave Mira, even for a moment.

"We must be practical Reena," he said, soothing her. "She's going to be all right."

119

He led her away, turned back to his children and gave a slight nod. 'Take care' it said, and the children acknowledged it with full hearts.

CHAPTER SIXTEEN

Veer had been trying to call Mira for the entire evening, and the entire night, but her phone seemed perpetually switched off. He tried leaving messages for her on various platforms, but they all went undelivered. For a moment, he thought that maybe she was upset with him over something, but as far as he could recall, they never really had any reason to fight lately.

The next day, he got up at the usual time for work and, the first thing he did, even before completely opening his eyes, was to check his phone for a message or call from Mira. But there was nothing, only two missed calls from his mother. He felt anxious, because nothing like this had ever happened before. He kept reminding himself that she was probably okay, that there must have been problems with the phone, or that maybe she had had to go somewhere urgently, and hadn't been able to inform him, but all these plausible explanations were squashed down by his palpitating heart, which kept insisting that something was wrong.

Veer's mind kept wandering back to the bad and the gory, leading him into further misery through unwanted speculation.

'Mira, Mira where are you?' he wondered.

Then, shaking himself to pragmatism, he uttered a short prayer for her safety, his hands folded in front of him.

The next hour was spent getting ready and fighting negative thoughts from his mind, along with perpetual glances at the phone, in hope of some news from her. It was while packing his laptop bag that his sister-in-law, came into his room with a big tray of breakfast, including everything from hot milk to fresh *paranthas* and sweetened curd. She was a young woman of seven and twenty winters down and had beautiful waist long hair, which she tied in a neat braided French plait at that moment.

Veer's brother, Sugreev had married his long-time sweetheart, Shipra, just a year ago and they both worked in Pune. She worked in the corporate sector, while his brother was a businessman, just on the brink of making it big. They were both were well acquainted with Mira, to the extent that they had invited her to their wedding, which of course she hadn't been able to attend, because it was an outstation wedding and Mira was never given permission to leave Delhi without her parents. But the four of them had been on various outings together, whenever Sugreev had come to Delhi to see his girlfriend.

"Shipraaaa!" screamed Sugreev from the other room. "You had better be dressed quickly, or else I'll be late," he said, as he came into the room where his wife stood feeding Veer, the *paranthas* dipped in curd.

"My, my, such love!" he exclaimed, and his wife blushed. "Where is Mira? I need her, for my sake, since you have devoted yourself to this fool." He walked over to the plate, rolled one of the *paranthas* and stuffed it down his throat in two overwhelming bites.

"Such terrible eating habits in the family," Shipra muttered to herself, looking at her husband and then at his paunch with a farfetched, disgusted expression. He gave her a mock kiss in return, his lips drawn into an extended pout.

Sugreev, patted his little brother on the back, as if jerking him out of his thoughts, "and what is the matter with you, Veer?" he inquired, "you don't seem to belong to this world."

Veer looked up at him, "Nothing," he replied, "it's just that Mira's phone has been switched off ever since yesterday evening, and no one is answering the landline as well."

Sugreev understood that his brother was more troubled inside than he showed on the outside, but then, they couldn't do much but wait. "Listen," he said, wanting to relieve his little brother of the stress, "she must have had to go somewhere with her family, and that is why no one is answering the landline."

Shipra put an arm around Veer, who was also a friend to her, and tried to lighten the situation, "Hey, don't worry," she said, "you're not like him," she motioned to her husband, "that you would so – grieve!" she smirked at the pun she had made on her husband's name.

It was one of her favourite jokes and the couple shared a good rapport with each other – easy in manners and abundant in love. After a moment of allowing the pun to seep in, they burst out laughing and Sugreev ran after his wife, chasing her away to the kitchen.

*

The entire day at office was nothing but a drag, a constant fight between thinking of Mira and struggling to pay attention.

Veer hated such days, when discrepancies with Mira affected other important aspects of his life. Of course, nothing was ever more important than her. This had been his usual problem, somehow, he seemed to derive concentration from the woman he loved and, when she was away, everything was away – the past month of his training had been so good, his seniors had praised him, he had been making good progress and, most importantly, he had had peace of mind, but just one day of miscommunication, or rather, lack of communication, had disrupted his routine and concentration.

Veer fidgeted with his phone, now and then, trying to call her, but receiving a dead end each time. At one point, one of his seniors caught him peering at his cell phone in the middle of an important task and, with a firm face, he motioned with his eyes to keep the phone away. But it was impossible to concentrate and, along with his mind, which did not currently contain a single positive thought, his heart gave way to a sinking feeling.

After numerous toilet breaks and incessant staring at the wall, his day was wrapped up in six to seven hours. Veer rushed home, determined to locate Mira at any cost. Moreover, there would not be anyone at home to disturb him.

*

Veer reached home around eight in the evening and rushed directly to his room. He had planned to call Mira's residence continuously, till someone finally answered, but after eight calls, of twenty rings each, he had to accept that all his efforts were in vain, and that there was nobody on the other side to answer the call.

He sat, tired and dejected, for a while. He had had only meagre meals that day and he felt weak inside, but he knew that his dejection was caused by his lack of communication with his beloved, Mira, and the thoughts concerning her well being that harrowed him.

He heard the turning of the key in the lock, his brother and sister-in-law were home from work, but he didn't feel like going out to greet them.

Shipra came straight to his room, as she saw the lights turned on. She looked a little dishevelled, as she had returned after eight hours of work in a stressful corporate environment. She was an intelligent woman who had pursued her MBA from the prestigious IIM Kolkata and she also handled the management of her husband's business. A multitasking woman from the early days of her marriage, she was known for balancing work and home and, in spite of her excellent educational qualifications, everyone knew her as very down to earth and amiable.

125

"Hey, how was your day? Any news from Mira?" she asked, peeping in through a partially open door.

Veer looked at her with dejected eyes and slowly shook his head. He was sitting on the floor in front of his bed, his phone lay on one side and he looked tired and unwell. She came up to him, her shoes making a tick tick sound as she walked across the room, and ran her hand over his head, feeling sorry and helpless for him, because nothing much could be done.

Both Sugreev and Shipra had tried calling their friends back in Delhi wondering if they had any news of Mira but no one could gather any information. It seemed as if Mira and her family had vanished into thin air, almost as wizards did. However, this was not a matter of fascination, rather, one of great concern.

"Hey," Shipra started softly, "you know you can only wait for her to call you and, when she does, make sure you scold her for being so irresponsible," she said, her eyes twinkling, wanting Veer to cheer up.

He looked up at her, trying to smile, but there were dark clouds of doubt spread over his face and he prayed in his thoughts, prayed to keep Mira safe and secure but, for some reason, his heart kept failing him. Veer was tired of waiting because it had been more than twenty-four hours since he had had any news of Mira and his eyes brimmed with tears. He turned away from Shipra, wanting to hide his emotions. He was choked and unable to speak. She sensed this and quietly walked out of the room, leaving him alone with his emotions.

Half an hour later, he heard his phone ring. It

sounded like a sweet melody, perhaps a nightingale's song. Veer hurriedly looked at his phone. But it wasn't Mira's call. His heart sunk for a moment, but then he realised that there was Ananya's name on the screen, Mira's sister. His mind was a potpourri of questions as he answered her call.

"Hello," said Ananya, hurriedly, her voice echoing as if she was calling from an empty hall or the washroom, "Hello, are you there?"

"Yes," he replied, his voice finding a way through the mesh of thoughts that had taken root in his mind.

"I need to talk to you. I hope you're not busy," she began, her voice seemed disturbed, as if she had been crying.

Veer interrupted Ananya's thoughts, unable to wait any longer. "Where is Mira? Is she okay? What happened?" he bombarded her with questions. His heartbeat was racing against time and he held on to the bed, in an attempt to prevent numbness from gripping him. His heart had been telling him that she was not okay, and he had been denying it, but Ananya's next words hit him hard. The way reality always hits a man, who has been trying to evade it.

"Mira has had an accident, J," Ananya said. She spoke carefully, addressing him as J, a derivative of *Jijaji* or brother-in-law as he would, eventually, be her sister's groom. Though this was usually used for fun, to tease Mira, but that day it was spoken in full sincerity. She stopped after that line, as if allowing time for the news to sink into his heart.

He sat stricken, as if literally, with an iron rod. "I knew something was wrong," he whispered feebly,

127

almost to himself, and then, louder, he said, "How bad is it? Is she all right?" Veer's hand was tapped on his heart, wanting it's pace to slow down as he came back to his senses.

"No," her voice was distorted and on the verge of breaking down. "She was hit by a speeding bus while coming home," she said, her voice barely escaping her lips and accompanied by sobs. "Mira is not okay, J. She hasn't regained consciousness for the past twenty hours." She stopped abruptly as if fearing to speak further.

Veer sat silently on the other side of the call. There were tears streaming down his cheeks, and his eyes were brimming with tears. He shut them to allow the full effect of the news to sink in. He was struggling inside. 'I told you she was in pain,' his heart interjected, 'no, you must remain calm,' his mind commanded.

"J," she began again, slowly framing the words as they fell from her lips. "I feel only you can make her all right. I know she will respond to you. I know she won't be gone for long, if you come to her side. I've seen how much she loves you..." she paused, overcome by tears, and waited for the choke in her throat to subside. "Will you please come?" she asked at last.

While she pleaded with Veer, he sat on the floor, in no condition to think and answer. Ananya, however, didn't stop at that, "If you won't come, they say... they say, if she doesn't come back in another ten hours or so, she'll lapse into a chronic state of unconsciousness," she blurted.

Veer was divided in his mind – one part was recreating his own version of Mira's accident and he cringed at the thought that she had got hurt, and must have been bleeding profusely. He remembered how much she feared dying in the hospital, all pierced and punctured with syringes, and another part of his mind was praying incessantly, 'Please God, please bring her back,' it said. 'Please don't take her away... She's mine,' and those last words reverberated in his head.

"J, are you there?" Ananya said, knowing that he must be having a hard time, but she couldn't help being impatient because he was the last hope she had.

"I'm coming," he asserted, staggering, but still struggling to regain control over himself.

Ananya hung up on the call without another word. She was hopeful that Veer would bring Mira back to life.

*

Veer didn't sit and brood. He couldn't, because there was no time. Mira was waiting for him. She needed him, his love, and he was going to retrieve her from that oblivion.

Mira was a seed he had planted in his life some years ago, and he wasn't going to let her slip into nothingness just like that, but at the same time, he was deeply grieved and worried. His prayers wouldn't stop. His body was trembling and his heart thumping against his chest. 'Slowly, slowly, please one thing at a time' he thought.

"Everything will be all right, I know she is going to be absolutely okay," he repeated to himself, his voice shaking but not his belief.

He had to think of a plan, book tickets, and take leave. 'No' his mind interjected. He must only think of getting to Mira. He rose to go to his brother, doing this alone was not possible and he needed help. When dealing with Mira, he possessed a weak heart.

Shipra and Sugreev were cooking dinner, something they preferred to do together, so that one person didn't feel the load of doing all the work. "*Baabu*, come over. The food is ready," he said, across the room, addressing Veer as he used to, in childhood. Sugreev soon realised that all was not okay. His brother's face bore a very troubled and gloomy expression. "Any news from Mira?" he asked.

The younger brother gave a slow nod, his head barely moving. What happened in the next ten minutes involved a retelling of Mira's accident, expressions of shock and tears from both Sugreev and Shipra, while Veer stood silently with tears rolling down his cheeks.

Sugreev stepped forward and took his brother in an embrace, hoping to soothe his pain a little. "Don't worry, just go there and take care of her. I'm sure she'll be fine," he said, as he patted his shoulders and stroked his hair with one hand. "Shipra, please look after the tickets. He can leave tonight and stay at Shourya's house," he continued, taking the reigns, as he felt the need to support Veer. "We don't have time to waste." Sugreev cupped his face in his hands as he spoke further, "you must be strong as she needs you." He looked into Veer's eyes, trying to transfer strength to him.

The next moment Shipra was swirling around in the house, booking tickets and helping Veer pack as well as trying to talk him out of anxiety. "You had better make sure that we get to talk to her, once she's all right," she said, on a lighter note, wanting to ease some of his stress.

He didn't respond, but he was listening as he packed furiously, wanting to see Mira as soon as possible. The wait, and the two hour journey, was going to be emotionally taxing. He was thinking about his beloved, who lay unconscious so many miles away, waiting for him to come to her. 'Please come back my love,' he prayed silently.

Veer was desperate to see her as soon as possible, but was also afraid of seeing her in that state, on the hospital bed. He was worried about how he would control himself on seeing her. Sugreev had suggested coming along, but he had refused, wanting to handle this alone. He could do it, and would do it, only for her sake. Though he had promised to go straight to his cousin Shourya's place, he knew he wouldn't be able to. He had decided to spend the night with Mira in the hospital.

*

Sugreev and Shipra returned home after dropping Veer off at the airport. They had been reluctant to leave him alone. They knew that a man's grief could be more overpowering to him than success, ambitions or even lust. Especially as their younger brother essentially functioned on his emotions and, regarding Mira, they were the most sensitive.

Just as his flight took off, Shipra broke down in front of her husband. "God, please make her all right and

131

give him strength," she prayed feebly as Sugreev took her away, his hands across her shoulders and his eyes shining with tears. He made the same prayer silently.

CHAPTER SEVENTEEN

A t one thirty in the night, Veer landed at the Indira Gandhi International Airport and took a cab directly to the B. L. Kapoor hospital. His journey had been a painful one because his memories of her, and images of her accident, had kept churning his head to pieces.

He had no idea how he would react to seeing Mira in such a state, and his tears would not stop gathering in the corners of his eyes. He struggled to keep the gloomy thoughts at bay. He wanted to think positively, but it was as difficult as holding one's breath underwater.

Principally, that was exactly how the human mind worked, the more we tried and eliminated negative ideas or thoughts, the more fiercely they clogged our system and barred us from positivity and contentment. The same was happening to Veer, but he didn't stop struggling. He had to focus his heart and his prayers on Mira.

He kept wishing to see her awake in the hospital, to see her chatting away cheerfully with her family members. He would take only a moment to look at her and, once satisfied that she was okay and back to normal, he would return to Pune and never let her know that he had been there to see her in that state.

133

But all that was only wishful thinking on his part, because the truth was that she lay in a deep slumber, fighting death with each step that he advanced towards her.

*

The moment Veer saw Mira in that pallid hospital room, he was caught in a tremor, and a seizure almost overtook him, as he saw his love, lifeless on the pale white bed. She had her head bandaged and there were dried patches of blood visible through the white of the bandage. Her left arm lay folded on top of her stomach, possibly a fracture. Tears rolled down from his eyes as he stood looking at her. She lay as if soundly asleep and lost in her dreams. The only sign of life was her breathing, her bosom heaving and the subsequent mist appearing on the inside of her oxygen mask.

He looked intently at his beautiful woman, her face scarred by the terrible accident, but to him she seemed to have gained an extraordinary glow on her face that made her radiant amidst all the gloom that pervaded the hospital room.

Of course, that wasn't what Veer saw, rather, what he imagined, because the next gaze upon her face showed him the daunting pallor of death and broke him to pieces.

"Dear God, please spare my love," he whispered, his breath creating a mist on the glass door through which he saw her. He dared not enter that room, at least, not at this hour, lest her parents asked him who he was. Whatever answer he gave would certainly mean trouble for Mira. No, he couldn't allow that, and decided to observe her from outside.

Veer peeped into the room through the glass, as far as his sight allowed, looking for someone staying with her for the night, but he couldn't see anybody. The couch meant for guests to sleep on was empty, though it was creased. He couldn't be sure of who had occupied it, and whether that person was still inside the room.

"Excuse me," he asked a nurse who was passing by, wiping his tears and nose as he spoke. "Please can you tell me who is staying with this patient," he spoke pointing to Mira.

The nurse looked him up and down, as if trying to read his expressions.

"I'm a friend," he blurted guiltily, lowering his eyes to the floor, "I don't want to bump into her parents, but I have to see her," he said, looking up at her with tear filled eyes.

The nurse's expression softened a bit and a smile spread across her face, a genuine smile, as she raised her arm to place it on Veer's shoulders.

"I think she needs you," she said very softly, looking intently at him. She nodded, opening the door for him to enter Mira's room. "Her mother is in the CT room," she added. "The doctor wanted to discuss her reports with the parents. Her father is also there, but you can see her for a moment," she explained, pressing his hand in a helpful manner as he looked at her with grateful eyes.

People like this always re-affirmed his faith in God, or in any other higher entity, which had preordained the life of men on earth. Veer smiled at the nurse and entered Mira's ward with soft steps. Of course,

135

he didn't fear waking her up; he would have played the drums for her, if loud sounds could wake her, but it was at the overwhelming grief upon seeing her closely, that his steps faltered.

He stood beside her bed looking intently at her. 'Can she feel my presence?' he thought as tears filled his eyes, his sight blurred by his own grief. He then sat on a stool next to her. Her lips seemed to tremble, but again, he was projecting his own imagination on to her.

He reached out for the hand that lay on his side of the bed and wrapped his palms around it. "Oh, my love," he whispered, the words barely escaping his lips, the emotions had been released, just one touch of her hand had been enough. "Please, come back love. Please come back!"

Veer buried his face in her neck, one arm crossed over her body as he cried his heart out, calling her to come back to him, his lips near her ears, whispering her name and evoking love. But no miracle happened, and Mira didn't stir even an eyebrow. After what seemed like only a moment, the rhythmic beep of the machine beside her was interrupted by a voice in the background, but it was muffled beyond recognition.

"Yes sister, I'll leave now," he managed to say, thinking it was the nurse who had come into the room, asking him to leave. But he couldn't let go of Mira's hand. How could he, she was his love and, certainly, he had all right to stay with her, and to look after her. He kept repeating "I love you, my love!" and "Please come back to me," but that elicited no response from Mira.

Veer's train of thought was brought to a halt by a hand that lightly touched his shoulders and he glanced behind him, standing up in horror, but still holding on to her listless hand. It was not the nurse who had interrupted him. In fact, that nurse was never seen again, during Mira's entire time at the hospital.

It was Mira's mother who stood behind him, looking at him with questioning eyes, eyes that were filled with tears, having heard the proclamations of his love for her daughter. She appraised him from top to bottom, stopping on his eyes, which were red and puffy from crying. She tried to recall his face from all the friends of her daughter, but she couldn't tell with any certainty who exactly he was.

Meanwhile, Veer stood frozen in his position. He had not wanted to cause more troubles for his beloved. He looked around the room, but there were no signs of Mira's father. Relieved, he returned to the mother. He could see that she bore a softened expression. She looked surprised, but not taken aback. It seemed to him as if she was trying to recognize him, maybe as one of Mira's friends. Without thinking twice, he let go of Mira's hand and bent down to touch her mother's feet, as propriety and respect demanded of a prospective son-in-law.

Mira's mother was further surprised and couldn't speak even a word. She simply stood gazing at him and observing his face, reading the emotions projected clearly through his eyes. 'He loves her,' she thought and she smiled at him.

Veer, on the other hand, was overcome with shame and confusion as he picked up his jacket and turned to leave. "I'm sorry," he said slowly, as he began to walk away, but then, he turned around abruptly and bent to kiss Mira on her forehead. He couldn't miss out on his love for fear of her parents. Without even attempting to look at her mother, he traced his steps out of the room. But a commotion behind him made him stop.

"Mira, Mira?" her mother exclaimed, running over to her.

As he turned around to see what had happened, he saw Mira's eyelids fluttering. A sudden joy rushed inside him and he ran to her, standing opposite her bed, tears streaming down his face, as he waited for her to open her eyes and look at him. In his mind, he was thanking God for answering his prayers, while her mother sat rubbing Mira's hands, waiting patiently for her to regain her senses. Being a doctor herself, she knew what this meant, and her face bore a relieved smile because she knew her daughter was safe now.

*

Mira slowly came back to consciousness, but opening her eyes seemed like Herculean task and there was a pounding pain in the back of her head. Her thoughts were blank. She only remembered the last thought she had had, closing her eyes on the road. Suddenly, all the emotions and thoughts hit her at once, and her brain churned images in front of her eyes – she remembered walking, crossing the road on her way back home, then, the sudden jerk, a strange feeling and the sound of her head hitting the ground. The last image was of a man running towards her, 'It's him,' she had thought, but of course, it couldn't have been Veer.

She focused her attention on the pounding in her head, which seemed as if blood was dripping inside her skull. As she tried to open her eyes, the light outside was too much, making it difficult. Her struggles were interrupted by a woman's voice calling out to her.

"Mira, Mira?"

It probably was her mother's voice. Did that mean that she wasn't dead? 'Why do my eyelids seem so heavy?' she thought, glad to hear her mother's voice, which gave her the needed energy and, at last, after what seemed like hours, Mira opened her eyes.

At first, she was blinded by the light. She tried to move her arm to block it, but that caused a sharp pain. Gradually, she became accustomed to the brightness and she saw a man standing in front of her. She moved her eyes over his face, studying his features – the black side swept hair, puffy, red eyes that had tears in them, soft, supple lips that were now curved into a grateful smile directed at her – at once the realisation struck her, filling her heart with joy. "It's him," she whispered to herself, tears surging from eyes. She was still figuring out if this was a dream or reality.

Veer smiled at her through his tears and ran his hand through his hair, he had an ardent wish to meet her lips with his own. After all, his beloved had come to life and he wanted to welcome her back with love.

Mira's mother sat back and silently observed her daughter and this boy. She was overjoyed to see the love they shared, to see a spark of life, light up in her daughter's eyes, as she looked at him, and to see the

139

smile on her face. It was all too overwhelming for the mother and, overcome with emotion, she wrapped her arms around her daughter. "Oh Mira," she heaved, "thank god!"

Mira suddenly shifted her gaze towards her mother. She hugged her back with an arm that barely moved, and tears escaped from the corner of her eyes. Her mother drew away, slowly, after a hearty and rather painful embrace. She struggled to come to terms with the presence of her mother and her lover in the same room, something which clouded her expression. She addressed her mother, looking worriedly at Veer with questioning eyes, but he wasn't concerned.

Veer was lost in observing the animation of life on Mira's face.

"Don't worry," said her mother aloud, "I understand." She motioned to him with her eyes, "he brought you back to life," she said, getting up and walking over to him.

Veer stood bewildered, as if he didn't trust his ears for what they heard.

Mira's mother took his hand and brought him closer to the bed. Then, in the typical Indian way, she placed her daughter's hand in his and smiled at both of them, acknowledging their relationship.

"Thank you, *beta*," she said to him, "you brought her back, when all of us had almost given up hope."

Mira smiled through her tears. She couldn't believe she was alive and it felt like heaven – her mother had accepted Veer without any questions. It was all too beautiful to be true. She looked up at her mother when she heard that he had brought her back to life, and wondered what that was supposed to mean. But her mother sensed her confusion and cleared her doubts.

"Mira, my love, God sent him to bring you back," said her mother, her voice all emotional and choked. "I know it was a miracle," she paused, remembering the moment. "The truth may be hard to believe, but the truth cannot change. The moment he kissed you, you were stirred back to life," she spoke as if enamoured by the thought of it, "I saw it with my eyes and Mira, which proves it, how much you both love each other. Then, who am I to oppose God's will?" she said, gifting Veer and Mira their happiest moment.

*

Veer left the hospital an hour later, around 4:00 a.m. because Mira was tired with all the happiness, pain and physical weakness. He left only when she was sleeping peacefully.

Before he walked out of the ward, her mother stopped him, "*Beta*, who informed you about her accident?" she asked.

"Ananya," he replied, his eyes lowered as he didn't dare to look his future mother-in-law in the eye.

She broke into a subtle smile. "So, they all knew," she said cheerfully, and he smiled to confirm it. "*Beta ji* sleep well, and don't hesitate to come back after some rest. I know Mira wants to see more of you." She looked proudly at him.

"Yes *Maa*," he said, and bent down to touch her feet,

141

leaving after the salutations.

*

The next few days were spent looking after Mira, as she gradually regained her health. She was discharged after a week, while Veer stayed with her for three days after she gained consciousness. She was physically weak from the bleeding inside, and needed a good rest for one to three weeks and, since her family was there to take care of her, they thought it appropriate for him to return and resume his training programme, in order to start his job as soon as possible.

The three days, however, had been an absolute delight for everyone, including Mira, who rejoiced to watch Veer and her mother talk animatedly to each other, as the future mother-in-law inquired about her future son- in-law's family, educational qualifications and plans for the future. This marriage talk was a little embarrassing for him and he blushed endlessly, while answering the typical marriage queries with complete honesty.

'How adorable!' thought Mira, as she lay back smiling and devouring each moment of her new life.

Every day, he would surprise her with a fresh bouquet of flowers to freshen up the surroundings, because that dull hospital ward otherwise smelled of medicines and naphthalene balls. Sometimes, he would bring a cake, and make Mira eat the bland hospital food, while the cake was distributed to the hospital staff because they had worked so hard to cure his beloved, and therefore deserved a treat. His kind-heartedness always touched Mira, and she smiled with tears in her eyes, as she observed how happy he was to see her all right.

The next day when Veer came to greet her, he had brought her a little locket, inscribed with the initials of both their names on a golden heart. Of course, he gave it to her when her mother was not around. But before that, as per Sugreev's instructions, he had to make Mira talk to both of them on a video call. She was overwhelmed to see them so emotional and caring towards her, especially Shipra *bhabhi* who had tears in her eyes all the while. They were so happy to see her all right and they were teasing him for being a cry baby all along, when they had been sure that Mira was going to be absolutely all right.

Mira's mother, too, was glad to see her daughter gelling well with her in-laws, especially the sister-in-law, since Indian families tended to give importance to such things, over the relationship of the bride and groom.

Thereafter, the next important thing was spending time together, and Mira's mother left the room soon after the video call ended, on the pretext of going to talk to the doctors and calling Mira's father and siblings to see her. As soon as she left the room, Veer stood up from his seat and kissed Mira on the forehead while she lay on the bed, her eyes closed. The entire morning she hadn't been able to sit up, because of the weakness that made her dizzy when she moved. He stood near her face, his eyes all filled with joy and he kissed her on both her eyes while she blushed, enjoying every moment.

"I think you should go back to your seat before *Maa* comes and catches us like this," she whispered in his ear, her eyes still closed. But, at the same time, she wanted more from him.

143

"It has been twenty-four hours since I saw you, and I haven't had my personal treat yet," he replied in the same whispering tone.

Mira opened her eyes and looked at Veer, as a smile spread across her lips. "Please kiss me," she whispered, reaching up towards him.

She had barely completed the sentence, when she felt his lips on hers and a stream of life rushed inside her, as she responded to him with equal vigour. He traced his hands across her body, holding her at the waist with one hand, the other placed behind her head, as if trying to support her and lifting her up, pulling her closer to him. Veer was infusing a new life in her with each grasp of his lips and each movement of his tongue which explored warm regions of Mira's mouth, while she let him go deeper and wider, exhaling and inhaling his vigour that worked as elixir for her, she didn't even need the oxygen mask, which had been inseparable from her for so long.

"You don't have to say please," he whispered to her, as she struggled not to let go of his lips, not allowing him to speak. He renewed the passion, their heartbeats rising and throbbing as they lay together, remaining suspended in their magic.

Time had lost track of them when they were interrupted by a knock on the door. They moved apart, blushing and grateful that it was only a nurse who had caught them in action.

The nurse entered the room hurriedly and avoided looking directly at them. "My, my, this isn't a foreign country," she blurted, pronouncing 'phoren' and 'cow-en-tree' in her own bizarre accent.

Veer and Mira tried to conceal a laugh, looking at each other with joy filled eyes, when the nurse gaped at her, "and look at you miss – sitting up in your bed, when morning you couldn't wake," she gasped, referring to the upright position in which Mira sat, while that same morning she had felt too weak to get up. "What did you do to this miss?" she asked him, her eyes playful.

Just then, Mira's mother came back into the ward and smiled to see her daughter radiant and sitting upright. She ran to them and studied the medical machines that were plugged into Mira's body.

"How do you feel?" she asked.

"Great!" Mira replied.

"Another miracle?" her mother asked, directing her question to Veer, her eyes mocking.

The young couple blushed, avoiding eye contact with her mother.

"Kind of," he replied, smiling at the floor.

The nurse coughed, to remind them of her presence. "May I collect samples for the test?" she asked.

Mira nodded, stretching out her arm for the nurse to draw blood.

"Oh, I forgot," her mother snapped, "Mira, your father is on the way with the other two," she said, addressing her daughter and then shifting her gaze to Veer. "*Betaji* it wouldn't be appropriate for you to meet her father here." She looked at him with entreating eyes, as if she were helpless and had no choice but to send him away.

145

"*Maa*," he said, smiling, "I totally understand. Please don't feel bad." He picked up his bag. "I'll come in the evening, okay?" he started to leave, "take care, love," he said and softly pinched Mira's cheeks before going.

Mira smiled at him and her gaze followed him out of the room. She didn't like the fact that he had to leave. She didn't want to see anyone else but Veer.

Her thoughts were interrupted by her mother. "Do you wish to lie down Mira?" she asked politely and Mira smiled back in answer, readjusting herself into a half lying position. "I'm sorry," her mother said, "I didn't like sending him away, but you know papa." She spoke slowly, holding Mira's hands as she continued, "you know, even we couldn't have found a better match for you," she said, smiling to see her daughter turn red in the face. "But why didn't you tell me before?" she spoke with her eyebrows knitted together, as if in a frown.

"Mummy," Mira explained, "you don't know how much I have wanted to tell you about Veer for the past five years. He's been on the tip of my tongue, but I couldn't muster the courage to tell you because of papa." She looked directly into her mother's eyes.

The elder lady smiled. "I like Veer. He's the best," she affirmed and Mira's heart made a momentary spin of joy.

The mother-daughter tête-à-tête was interrupted by the arrival of Mira's father, along with her two siblings. Naturally, they were more than overjoyed to see her in a better form and even her father was so overwhelmed that he ran up to her to wrap her in his arms, something he had not done in a very, very,

146

long time. The moment he held her in his arms, she felt a sudden rush of emotion in her. She was not used to such expression of love from her father and it made her feel guilty for thinking badly of him, especially because Veer had left the room through fear of him. This unforeseen hug that Mira received from her father let go of an entrapped ocean of delight in her.

A similar reservoir of love had also been released in the heart of her father, following the traumatic accident of his beloved child, he had begun to appreciate the little nuances of life that involved treasuring affection, manifesting in their family a new meaning of love. This transition in Mira's father, from the head of the family to the father figure, was appreciated by all the members of the family, and especially by Mira, because she was the focus of his affections. Though they shared the same conflicts as before, and still differed in their intellectual understanding of what they wanted from life, the feelings of hostility that each of them had harboured for the other were suddenly transposed to feelings of love and understanding. She was in tears when her father let go of the embrace and, unable to bring his emotions to fruition, he merely ran his hand over her head.

Next were, Ananya and Aditya who took turns to embosom their eldest sister, looking at her with moist eyes but no words to say. What could they say, when everything had been so overpowering? But they had been relentless in their belief that Mira would be all right. Still, the face-off with death had been too much for them to bear. Being younger to Mira, both of them had always looked up to her, more as a friend than as an elder sister, and they shared all kinds of secrets with each other, secrets sworn to

147

death.

The youngest of them, Aditya, was deeply attached to her and shared all his thoughts and wishes with her – like the fact that he loved music and wished to become a professional drummer. But, a profession so out of the box was unlikely to be accepted in a household like theirs, and it was incognito that Mira had saved money with Veer, to get Aditya enrolled in drumming classes. They had heard him play at his school festival, and he was possibly the best, but nothing came easily in life. Born to an IAS officer and a doctor, Mira and her brother had vocational callings, with one wishing to be a writer and, the other, a drummer.

Only Ananya was pursuing something respectable, in the eyes of their parents, because she was studying medicine. She, having read a lot about medical cases where patients were revived from their death beds through prayers and love, had hoped that calling Veer, would help Mira regain consciousness and, without thinking twice, she had done what was needed.

Both Ananya and Aditya stood beside their elder sister, eyeing her suspiciously, with a smirk on each of their faces, because they knew what had cured her - and they intended to tease her about it for days. Their mother stood at a distance, watching them, while she and their father discussed Mira's reports with the doctor.

"So the magic of Prince Charming worked for you, right?" chirped Anu, elbowing her sister gently, her eyes dancing with a certain light as Mira blushed and held her hands in understanding. "You must thank me, for I saved your life," she continued,

148

feigning smartness, only to end up laughing together.

"You didn't! Someone else did..." interrupted Aditya his voice sounding more like a bass less drum because he was so overcome by emotion. "And you know," he continued earnestly, as if he were about to tell her something important, "we met Veer while coming upstairs." He lowered his voice towards the end, lest their parents should overhear.

Mira's expression tensed at the thought of her father having noticed him.

"No, don't worry," Aditya said. "We just smiled at each other and, I must say, he looked rather happy."

The doctor announced himself to the three youngsters, smiling and looking pleased with the report. He was cute, but also balding in some places and he always wore a certain expression of cheerfulness, especially while talking to their patients and, all together, it made him quite funny to look at.

"Good morning, young lady!" he began, addressing Mira with the same peculiar expression, "I can see that you're as fit as a fiddle. What's the secret, *haan*?" he smiled knowingly as she tried not to laugh. The suffixed Hindi word '*haan*' at the end of an English statement was a common way of talking in India, especially among people who considered Hinglish to be a language in itself.

"So, your internal bleeding has stopped and, trust me, I don't know how," he said, finishing his statement while looking at Ananya. Everyone had noticed that he had a keen eye for her.

She turned away, looking at Mira as if requesting help. 'Save me!' her expression said. She was afraid that the doctor would start asking her medical questions again, which she wouldn't be able to answer, but then, she hadn't got any wrong yet.

This time, however, the doctor didn't ask any and he spoke to Mira directly. "But, young lady, you need a lot of rest, no more walking on the roads with your eyes closed!" He was hoping to be funny, but nobody else laughed.

Mira's father could be seen muttering something with a distorted face, as if he was abusing him for making a stupid joke out of his daughter's life. On his part, he had made sure that the drunk DTC driver who had struck Mira would have a hard time getting out of jail, and this doctor, too, was going to have it from him.

After the doctor left, Mira observed her mother and father discussing something in hushed voices, as she lay back on the bed to rest. Maybe they were discussing her health, but she was not concerned with the content of their discussion, rather, she couldn't help noticing the proximity of her parents – how close they seemed to each other, almost as one, not merely as husband and wife, but as one united entity. This thought brought a smile to her face; and she could sense the charm in their eyes as they talked to each other. For a moment she couldn't believe it. She couldn't understand this spark between them, something she had never seen before, at least never so strongly. She couldn't stop staring at them. When her father touched her mother's face lightly with his fingers, maybe in the act of explaining something to her, there was a knowing smile on the daughter's face and she made a silent prayer.

"Thank you, God, for showing us this day," she whispered.

Indeed, it was a great day for their family, a day they had longed for, and now cherished. 'If one accident could bring about so many positive changes, then I'm glad it happened,' thought Mira, smiling as she closed her eyes and allowed sleep to capture her.

CHAPTER EIGHTEEN

*T*ring Tring... Tring Tring

"Hello," Veer answered the call.

"Hi! Where are you? When will you be reaching the New Delhi station? Please tell me ASAP," Mira said, all at once.

"What?" he questioned, "What about the station? Where are you?"

"I'm waiting for you at the station, my love. Actually, I have something very important to share with you, and I couldn't wait for tomorrow, so I came to receive you," she chirped. "Now, tell me what time will you be reaching the station? Here on the platform, it says 15 minutes, but I want to know exactly."

But there came no reply.

"Hello? Can you hear me?" she shouted into the phone.

"I'm not coming today," Veer replied shortly.

"W-h-a-t? But, didn't you tell me you were returning on Saturday?"

"I'm sorry I couldn't inform you about the change in

schedule." He paused for some seconds and then spoke, "I... I will be reaching the station tonight at 11:00 p.m. and, of course, you won't be able to come and receive me that late."

"Oh, but that's not fair!" She sounded disheartened, but she was glad that he hadn't extended his trip for very long. She would get a chance to see him the next day, and she would tell him then.

"I'm sorry love... I'm sorry."

Mira could sense that something wasn't right. His tone was too flat and dry, lacking the usual spark he had always had while talking to her. "Are you all right?" she asked. "Has something happened?"

"No, I'm fine, just... just a bit of fever and headache. I'll be fine," he replied in a soft voice.

"Why do you always do that?" she said, exasperated and restless to hear him in pain, "Why can't you get enough sleep at home?"

"It's okay, trust... trust me, and I'm fine. It's just, like going to sleep, I mean I don't want to sleep... I mean please let me sleep."

"Okay, okay, my love, you may sleep, I won't disturb you," she said, deeply worried about this young man, whose voice gave away so clearly that something wasn't right. "Take care, okay?" she said.

Veer disconnected the call.

To Mira, her beloved meant more than the world. She sensed that he wasn't okay, but for some reason she didn't call him back to bombard him with questions, like she always did, nor did she harrow him into swearing their personal 'Swear-on-our-love' to find out why he was not his usual self. She simply retraced her steps towards the metro station, to board a train back home. Though she had been reading a copy of Dostoevsky's *Notes from the Underground,* her mind kept wandering back to the conversation they had just had and she couldn't stop herself from sending him a text message,

"Baby, I know you must be asleep by now, but I could feel that there was something wrong. Don't worry, I'll make everything all right tomorrow. Love you my husband <3"

The 'husband' was deliberately included, because they were going to be married soon enough.

Text sent.

Text delivered to Veer.

*

Mira reached home thinking about Veer and the situations that were favourably developing, regarding their marriage. She had finally been able to convince her father to meet him, at least once. Since her father was strictly against the idea of a girl seeking a life partner on her own, especially when he was not of the same caste. These things became impossible when the girl happened to be his own daughter. But, with God's grace, he had been mellowed into meeting this person once, because his daughter had assured him that she would not marry Veer if he found even one genuine fault in him. That being the case, her father had agreed. Though he himself was a highly egoistical man, Mira believed that her father would love the man who had swept his daughter of her feet.

154

This was the news that she couldn't wait to tell Veer, but one thought kept drawing her away. 'What was the matter with him?' 'Maybe, he really wasn't well,' she thought, but then he had gone home to his native place in order to see his parents and attend some religious functions, so what could have gone wrong? 'No' she jerked her head, 'if something had been the matter, he would have told her.' After a long debate about what could or could not be, she finally rested on the idea that he definitely wasn't well. She decided to go meet him at his place the next day.

The next morning was a bright Sunday and Mira, who was usually a late sleeper, woke up at 8.00 a.m. because she had to go meet Veer. She lied at home, saying that there was some meeting in college and, now that Mira was a working woman, a professor at Miranda House, Delhi University, her parents didn't really nag her about her whereabouts like they had before. She got ready and was out of the house by 9.30 a.m. She knew he would be asleep, so she decided to surprise him by paying an unexpected visit.

Dressed in his favourite red *kurti*, black trousers and stilettos, her hair partially tied back and partially wet, dark kohl in her eyes and a dab of red lipstick, she was all set to make him blush first thing in the morning. She took her usual route to his house, the usual bus, and reached his area by 10.30 a.m.

For some reason, her heart was palpitating uncontrollably as she paced towards his house. She couldn't make out the sense of oblivion that was enveloping her. It was something she could feel but not see. She brought a rose on the way, as she sometimes did, just to see him blush, the way he always did when she bought surprises for him.

155

She reached his house, and with each step of the three flights of stairs, she could feel something descending inside her. She reached his room. The door was open, but he wasn't inside. In fact, there wasn't anybody in the house, only a mess of clothing sprawled across the bed. She tried calling him, but his phone lay on the bed, ringing. She went upstairs and found him on the roof.

Veer was sitting on the floor, with his head ducked between his knees. The moment he heard her coming, he looked up, but what Mira saw in his face was something she hadn't seen before and she could not comprehend it. His eyes were red and swollen, as if he hadn't slept for days, he was unshaven, unwashed. His eyes looked into hers, begging an apology, but she didn't even notice that note of apology, for she was too concerned about his health.

Teary eyed, without speaking, she held his hand and brought him down to the room, closing the door behind her. She did not want any disturbances. She only wished to know the reason behind his weariness and despair. Gently, she made him sit down on the bed and kissed his eyes. The moment her lips touched the closed eyelids, streams of tears began rolling down his cheeks. She could bear anything but to see him cry. Choked with her own emotions, she asked, "What is the matter?" in the softest voice.

Veer didn't look up at her, but put his arms around her waist, brought her closer and rested his head against her stomach, his tears creating wet patches on her red cotton *kurti*.

Mira held him tight and, again, mustered the strength to ask, "Please, tell me what happened?"

156

He took some time to answer, gathering the courage to tell her something, something that would be the greatest blow to her, that would shatter her to pieces. Those pieces, which he, himself, had healed and put back together. Now, the same man was about to tear them apart. He had lost her, forever. He had lost his life, forever, and there was no way he could bring it back. "I'm... sorry," he muttered feebly, unable to bring himself to say anything further.

She kept stroking his hair with her fingers, gently mellowing him, while emotions and thoughts rushed into her own mind, regarding what could have happened and why Veer was in so much pain.

"I'm so sorry... I'm sorry... Please forgive me..." he began, breaking down in a heavy sob.

This frightened her terribly. She had never seen Veer, so upset and wretched. He was always under control. He kept everything under control, for her. Always. He had always been the epitome of 'everything is all right' and, suddenly seeing him like this made her lose her wits. She freed herself of his hold, held his face to her level, her eyes fiery and red, tears trickling down, as she pierced into his eyes, and further into his soul. "Tell me!" she demanded.

"I've lost you forever," he said, almost as a reaction, and then, breaking into sobs, "I've broken our promise, our promise of love, irreparably..." he continued, "I have sinned against you Mira, I have broken your trust."

She let go of his face, unable to comprehend the words she had heard him say or decide whether she heard him correctly. She sat down on the floor, because she feared she would black out. She often

157

had in the past, and she felt that same dizziness now, as if all the blood was rushing down her head.

One thing kept indicating that something had broken inside Veer, that he was telling the truth – never, in six years, had she seen him so weak and shattered. There was a sense of finality in the way he said 'Mira'. It felt like the breaking of a bond. She took time to come to terms with this, as she anticipated the oncoming disaster, the impending doom that was to unleash against her soul.

Mira slowly settled down to sit next to him and he reached for his phone, nervously, his hands shaking uncontrollably. He unlocked the phone and showed her a picture of a very beautiful girl.

She looked at the picture intently, taking his phone in her hand with trembling fingers and observing the person in the picture very closely. The girl in the photograph had a very plain oval face, with her hair tied back in a long ponytail, and reddish pink spots around the corners of her cheeks and clear black eyes. She wore a white and orange s*alwar kameez* in the picture, and matching bangles. At one look she seemed like a simple, ordinary girl, but a closer introspection Mira realised that she had no legs, only thighs, and that is where her body ended, just after the torso. She was beautiful at first sight and, pure at heart, seemingly. Mira held his phone in her trembling hands, fearing whatever truth, he was about to reveal. "Who is she? What happened to her?" she asked, meekly.

Veer looked at her and grief descended upon him like the pallor of death.

"Is she okay?" Mira asked, clouds of doubt in her

158

eyes.

He nodded a slow and sad nod.

All this while, she knew, he had been gathering the courage to let it all out, to tell her, and now, whatever burdened him inside was about to come out. She could see his pupils contracting and dilating, she could feel his heart thumping against his chest, and she could feel the lump in his throat trying to choke him, just when he wanted to speak. How well she had come to know every inch of him in the past six years of their relationship.

"Mira," he began, "this young woman is now my responsibility." He stopped, the tears, and maybe, his own emotions, made it difficult to continue. "I've promised her parents that I would sacrifice all, sacrifice all to look after her," he spoke after a pause, sobbing by the time he finished speaking.

For a moment, it was hard for Mira to make out what he was mumbling. She wanted to know the exact nature of this responsibility, which had been entrusted to him. "Please tell me everything clearly! Why are you so upset? What kind of responsibility? What do you mean, Veer? Please speak!" burst Mira, all at once, begging and commanding in the same tone.

"I have married her."

Mira's heart was throbbing out of her chest and her breath was quickening. She needed to hold on to something. This was all too much. She was about to black out. Somehow, she held on to Veer, to her reality.

159

"What?" she spoke, eventually, slowly coming to terms with whatever was happening to her. The words had barely escaped her lips, but they managed to reach Veer.

"She's my wife now," he continued, a little more in control of himself, now that the truth was out in the open. Now he could focus on Mira's face, watching her break apart on the inside. Her eyes were as red and her nose, something that had always been the cynosure of his attention, stood red on her tear soiled face. He observed that little mole on her upper lip, barely visible to others, but he knew exactly where it was. He noticed that lazy strand of her hair that was forever out of place. He noticed her, as if visually devouring her for the last time. "Mira," he mumbled feebly.

Mira looked up at Veer and asked him, "Then who am I?"

He had no answer. On the inside, her broken soul was finally beginning to fall apart. She grieved to see him have no answer, but she mustered the courage to speak to him, because she was not going to accept this.

"Listen, love, please tell me that all this is not true! It's not possible, you're... You're mine... We were about to get married, right? Don't we love each other?" She became more frantic with each thought, as fresh tears gushed up to her eyes, only to roll down her face once again, "you love me? Tell me... Tell me YOU LOVE ME!" she shrieked, begging him, holding on to him, both physically and emotionally.

Veer stood with his eyes lowered, with teardrops on his eyelashes. Tears were going to be inevitable companions, from that day onwards.

Mira stopped. There was no reason for him to joke about something so serious, not with her. It was beyond doubt. He would never joke about marrying someone else, but Mira wanted something to cling on to, to disprove the present. How could she believe that the man standing in front of her, who was going to be her partner for life, could suddenly turn into a stranger? How could she let go of him? How could she give up on the sole reason of her existence, the other half of herself? She couldn't. What about him? How could he eliminate her soul from his heart? No, this couldn't be true. Her life couldn't come to a halt so abruptly.

She delved deeper into his eyes, searching, penetrating his soul and, in an instant, she knew that all was over.

At last, the final blow – Veer's wedding photograph. Mira refused to take the phone in her hand. She refused to touch anything that belonged to him. She wanted to get out his apartment, away from those walls that seemed to be closing in on her. That apartment, which had been so familiar once, suddenly seemed strange to her. Even the bed, 'his' bed now, and not 'their bed' which had once been the witness to their union, suddenly seemed unfamiliar to her.

'Relationships are so fragile,' she thought, her head caught in a surge of memories, questions, also horror. She wanted to know what had made Veer do this, she wanted him to trample her, maybe even kill her, because life without him was null and void. She tried to focus on the picture, tears blurring her sight, she couldn't believe it was him, standing next to this

161

other woman, tied to her in matrimony. No doubt, the woman looked very beautiful in the picture, though her eyes seemed empty. Veer, on the other hand, had the pallor of despondency on his face, even in the picture.

Mira could understand that her beloved had literally sacrificed himself in the match and she realised how burdensome it was for him to be in the wrong, making him vulnerable from both sides. He had taken a stand for the right, yet wronged someone back home. But, had he stood up for Mira, he would have wronged this woman, and himself, as a moral individual.

Veer was looking intently at her, as she surveyed the picture through watery eyes. Gradually, he began narrating how it had all come to pass. He told her how, unwillingly he had had to take such a drastic step, how he had been trapped between the right thing to do and his love for Mira. How he had knowingly sinned against her.

CHAPTER NINETEEN

It was a bright sunny day and Veer could feel the gushes of wind brushing across his face, mixed with the peculiar smell of the railways and the chaos of the approaching platform. He stuck his head out of the door, carrying his bag on the shoulders and saw his father standing in the middle of the heavy crowd, looking for him through the coaches of the of the train, as it slowly came to a halt at the platform. He alighted and went straight towards his father, tapping his shoulder from behind.

"Papa," he said as his father turned around to see his dear son's face with misty eyes,

"*Beta*," exclaimed his father, choked with emotions. He grasped his son in a long and tight embrace. Veer bent down to touch his father's feet and seek blessings, after which they both began to walk towards the exit, chatting happily with each other.

Veer and his father shared an exceptional bond. Though they rarely got to see each other, maybe once in six months, no distance could separate the attachment they had for each other. Theirs was the kind of bond that Mira longed to have in her family, a bond based on respect for each other and love

163

towards each other. She used to laugh whenever he told her how he had loved to sleep between his parents, with his feet on his father's chest and she would cherish the fact that she was to have them as her future family.

The father-son duo shared a common passion for cars and driving and it was believed, in their family, that no one could drive as smoothly as his father, and that Veer, of course, had taken after him. That day, his father drove them home, chit chatting all the way and enjoying the thirty minutes they had to themselves on the ride back home.

"Papa there was no need for you to come all the way. I could have managed, you know that," he said, trying to hold a screwed up face against his bursting mischievous smile, "you ruined my surprise!"

"*Beta*, I wanted to talk to you about something important, that is why I thought I'd come and receive you at the station," his eyes danced brightly, focussed partly on the road and partly on his son.

"*Papaji*, I, too, have something really important to tell you," said Veer, in a squeaky voice, as he thought of Mira and blushed.

"All right, you first," said his father.

Veer, however, couldn't speak about Mira, all of a sudden, so he let his father go first. His father was a very plain man who worked as an officer in a government bank and led a life of satisfaction. Though he was the head of the family, as is the case in patriarchal societies, he never asserted that kind of authority and control over his family. He believed that love was the answer to all problems. Hence, he was a greatly revered person in his family, and even outside it. There was one aspect of his character that was really special, and that was the way he dealt with children, especially his own children. Never had he reprimanded them for not scoring good enough marks in their examinations or, for that matter, for failing them completely. But as a father, he had never failed to instil the right values in them.

"*Beta*, do you have any girl in mind?" asked his father, quite abruptly, sounding excited.

Veer blushed deeply before replying, his cheeks the colour of strawberries beneath his light beard. "Sorry papa, but for whom?" he spoke as he drew out a poker face, wondering whether his mother had spilled the truth to his father.

"For me!" exclaimed his father, suddenly bursting into laughter, "of course, for you *beta*," he said at last, smiling in the most understanding way a father could.

"Umm, yes papa," he blurted, trying to overcome the embarrassment of talking to his father about his girlfriend.

"Yes?" teased his father.

"Yes," he replied, very quietly, looking down at his feet, as if trying not to feel the overpowering reality of this interview with his father.

"Mira?" asked the father, all of a sudden, looking straight at his son while driving, something he hardly ever did. He was usually focused only on the road, but that day was different.

Veer was sure that the source of information was his

mother, and the blush on his cheeks was too obvious to conceal. He squeaked out a small "yes," barely audible to his father. At last he simply smiled at his father, a smile that spelled out, 'Yes, papa, I want to marry Mira'.

"She teaches, right?" his father continued with his interrogation, enjoying every moment of it, when his son could only reply in shakes and nods. "Well, I hope you have thought about it. I mean I don't doubt your choice, but you know, another teacher in the family! You don't know how hard it is to handle teachers," his father broke into a wicked smile, referring to his wife. "Ask me about it, thirty-seven years I have spent with an English teacher, and now you wish to bring home a Professor of English?" he spoke as his eyes gleamed with laughter.

"Papa, I love you so much!" was the only thing his son could manage to say, smiling inwardly at the situation, which his father had made so light and easy going for him.

Veer looked raptly at his father driving the car, his lips bent into a small smile that was a residue of the hearty laugh they had just had. Oh, how he adored his father, absolutely adored him, and why not? He had only one idol and that person was his father. He noticed the spark in his father's eyes, maybe a glint of approval regarding Mira, something that satisfied him greatly. He noticed the grey brown hair and beard of his father, that one signature cap he always wore, which hid most of his head and neck, but what he noticed most profoundly was the old age that was setting in on his father and there developed a sudden rush of emotion inside him as an old childhood fear gripped him once again.

"Papa, I'm sorry," he said, suddenly guilty and in regret of all the time he had spent away from his father, because he was busy creating a better life for himself.

His father took the apology to be directed in the context of Mira and he looked at his son with proud eyes, running his left hand over his head and embracing him with love and blessings. "I trust you completely my son," he said.

*

The next two days passed in happiness, with family and childhood friends. Veer's elder brother, Sugreev and his wife Shipra had come all the way from Pune with their little one, who was almost a year old. The intention had for everyone to get together, but foremost, the gathering was to help him advocate about Mira.

"No, no, you have to marry the girl of our choice. Also, your Mira is of a lower caste and I don't want a lower caste daughter-in-law, you better keep that in mind," rattled Veer's mother, repeating this monologue for the nth time.

She was the only one left to convince, partially because there were times when she agreed, but then there were times when influenced by other gossip mongers, and refused to acknowledge the relationship.

"*Maa*, she isn't a lower caste. Don't create stories in your head," said the elder brother, angered by his mother's reproach on such menial grounds.

"I have one idea!" interrupted his father, "See, I am in

favour of Mira and so is everyone else, except you," he said, addressing his wife, "So, by majority voting, Mira is approved as our daughter-in-law, and that should be considered."

He ended with a look of naughty triumph on his face. He knew his wife would eventually give in. There stood no reason to reject Mira.

But Veer was reluctant to force his wishes upon his mother, so he went up to her and held both her hands in his, in order to begin his entreaty.

"*Maa*, do you know why I like Mira so much?" he said, not able to say 'love Mira' in front of his mother, and thereby settling for like. "It is because she is so much like you, and I know that only a perfectly balanced lady like you can handle me, this somewhat dyslexic son of yours," he added, with eyes filled with tears and lips drawn into a subtle smile because he knew that mother was half appeased.

"*Maa*," he continued, "you will be surprised to see how Mira is always concerned with her books like you have been, how she will be worried about the education of our children like you have always been about yours, how she will teach them to respect and care about books and education like I have always seen you do." Veer spoke with misty eyes, because he knew that he was spelling out his dream to his mother. "*Maa*, I will be the luckiest man in the world to have a woman, so much like my mother, as my wife."

That was enough to satisfy his mother and, slowly, she gave the final nod, her eyes brimming with tears.

*

The room was filled with smoke from the burning of the incense sticks. Veer had come to pay worship to his ancestral gods in the temple. They say that Fate is the only inevitable, and it often bowls you a googly at the most unexpected times.

It was through that film of smoke that Veer saw Saanjh for the first time. He was struck, immediately, by her beauty, which featured two large fish shaped eyes and jet black hair, oiled and neatly combed into a braid. She had a sharp protruding nose, very different from Mira's barely visible that had always driven him crazy, with its superimposed cuteness. Saanjh was seated on a chair and busily engaged in talking to her friends. Dressed in a white and yellow *salwar kameez,* she looked hardly more than sixteen or seventeen years of age.

Veer was surprised at himself. He was checking out this other woman, so closely and intently. What business did he have, checking out a woman other than his Mira? But for some reason, he could not help looking at her and it was only when she moved away from her friends to head towards the main temple area did he realise that Saanjh had not been sitting on just any chair, rather, it was a wheelchair that she used to get around. He discerned later, that the beautiful and innocent girl did not have the privilege of legs, beyond the thighs, something that filled him with disgust at the suffering and unfairness of the world.

It was later that he learnt from his father that this young girl, Saanjh, was an orphan, who lived with her father's younger brother and his family.

Just like Mira, Veer too was greatly affected by the sufferings of other people and he often ended up feeling sympathetic towards them. For now, he couldn't help noticing how she manoeuvred across the room on the wheelchair, without even a flicker of pain or frustration on her face, distributing sweets to everyone present. The moment it was his turn, she looked straight into his eyes and gave a warm smile. It was at that moment that their fates were sealed.

"Why were you staring at me like that?" Saanjh asked, once they had developed a good friendship, something which took no longer than a few minutes.

"I was wondering," Veer began, "where you get so much courage from?"

"When God withholds something, he gives you something else to compensate for it, and how you use that something is what makes you special," she said, her eyes bright and sparkling with a look of absolute contentment.

"Your spirit is enviable Saanjh," he said, "don't ever let that crumble. It's the most beautiful thing about you."

"Thank you," she blushed, "you are really pure hearted, you know. I get those vibes," she continued in her vernacular language. "May I tell you something? But you must promise to keep it a secret!"

Veer nodded as his lips broke into a curious smile.

"I am about to get married soon," she said, allowing a full blush to overcome her cheeks, rendering them adorably pink.

"That's great news! When is the big day?" he asked, wondering who had the honour of loving her.

"I must not reveal everything now, but his name is Sooraj," she chirped, "it's an arranged marriage, but I am so excited, you know, I always wanted to get married!" she spoke, her eyes brimming with dreams.

Veer returned a heart warming smile to her. He was happy to know that people still had humanity left in them and he was greatly impressed by this man called Sooraj. He congratulated her on the good news and Saanjh rolled her wheelchair away, to hand more sweets out to the others, happy and satisfied that she had found a good friend.

"All the best," he called after her, turning to move out of the smoke filled room and head home for the delicious lunch his mother had prepared.

CHAPTER TWENTY

It was two days later that Veer heard the news. He was playing with his little nephew and chatting with Shipra, while she prepared bottles of milk for the infant. The next moment he heard the maid running around the house looking for his mother and shouting frantically, "*Bibiji, Bibiji*" but his mother was not at home, so the Shipra answered her call.

"*Anarth ho gya,*" she went on, "Something terrible has happened!" She was crying and howling, making her words gibberish.

"Saanjh *beti* has tried to commit suicide," she blurted.

It was shocking news, especially for Veer, because just two days ago, he had been so impressed by Saanjh's spirit. He rushed out of the room, the baby still in his arms, trying to nibble away the edges of his shirt collar with newly formed teeth. He just couldn't believe what he had heard. "Is she okay?" he asked the maid.

She nodded, her eyes full of tears and, at once, he knew that there was more to the situation. A woman, who had been so full of happiness in the temple, two

172

days ago, would not just choose to end her life all of a sudden. She had told him that she was going to get married soon, so what could have happened? His mind pondered over a number of things that could have happened, compelling her to take such a drastic step. Maybe her engagement, with Sooraj, had been broken, or maybe she had been feigning the charm and radiance he'd seen the other day. No, the positivity in her eyes and the way she had spoken were too natural.

'I must find out,' Veer thought, 'and maybe help her if I can,' he decided to go and find out the cause of such extreme measures.

"*Bhabhi* you stay here and take care. I'll find out what has happened," he said, in a voice controlled and understated, handing the baby to his mother, and rushing out of the door, towards Saanjh's house.

Saanjh's paternal uncle was a close friend of Veer's father, because they belonged to the same clan and worshipped the same deities, so they were often seen together at the temples, in public places or at each other's house.

Saanjh was an orphan, who stayed with her paternal uncle, his wife and their two sons, who were both younger than her. Her aunt was very fond of her and had reared her as her own daughter. She had been determined to find a treatment for Saanjh's medical problem, so that someday, she would walk, but, in spite of spending a lot of money, consulting doctors across India, there was no hope for a treatment to make her walk. A prosthetic leg could support the entire body, if the other leg was normal, but, with two prosthetic legs, balancing the human body would be an unimaginable task. So, Saanjh would have to

173

stick with the wheelchair, for ease of movement, something which did not bother her because she was comfortable in her body and disliked going to doctors.

Saanjh and her loving family had stayed in Gwalior before coming to that place, a few years ago, which was why Veer did not remember her from his youth. She was twenty years old, but she looked very young, almost seventeen.

Her uncle and aunt had arranged her marriage to a shallow, twenty-five year old man, Sooraj, who had a small business of his own. He had not seemed like one who would wish to marry a disabled woman, and love her all his life. But, even though her uncle and aunt suspected that the young man had agreed to marry Saanjh, only for the great dowry she would get, they chose to turn a blind eye to it, because they were ready to replenish their daughter with money every time, if that was the cost for her to lead a normal, happy life.

Saanjh, who had always had an optimistic approach to life, had been looking forward to a new beginning, and a loving partner in Sooraj. Though her body would make it difficult, she still hoped to achieve femininity and she had often pondered over her sexuality. She had wondered whether she would ever be able to experience those intimate moments with a man, and she decided, on her part, to love her husband in every possible way and explore the limitations of her body with him by her side.

Little did she know, that she would be forcibly pushed to those limits, before marriage, that too by her fiancé, Sooraj.

Driven crazy by the thought that his masculinity would go waste if he married a cripple girl, her would-be husband had decided to test her, not for her virtues, but for sexual satisfaction. In his mind, it was simple – if she wouldn't consent, then he would force his way through her, both literally and metaphorically. Nobody could say anything, because she was engaged to him. In fact, he never contemplated anyone getting to know about it. It was a husband and wife matter, and nobody had any say in it except him, not even the wife.

When Veer reached Saanjh's house, which was just two blocks away, he saw a huge crowd of people gathered outside, inside, and around it, doing nothing but staring and talking about the great show of drama and tragedy.

When the real horrors were explained to him by the bystanders, regarding the reason behind the young woman's suicide attempt, tears filled his eyes and he felt a surging anger inside him. He couldn't believe that people could be so heartless and inhuman to the poor girl.

Saanjh had been raped by Sooraj, who had left her lying near the lake. Though she fought with all her might, scratching his face and ears, she had caused him enough damage, but still he had overpowered her, ruining her life. It was only after total defeat that she had tried to drown herself as she had come to terms with reality.

Veer wanted to hunt down that beast and make him pay for his sins, but first, he was drifting towards Saanjh, who sat on a '*charpoi*', surrounded by a number of ladies, her paternal uncle and aunt, who held her in a tight embrace. She had been saved

175

from drowning by a passer-by, who had brought her home as a lifeless mass of flesh. She had been revived physically, but her lifeless eyes spoke of the horror and pain she had been through.

Everybody else's eyes were red and tired by the continuous gushes of tears, that were a constant come and go, but Saanjh's eyes were dry, with not a single tear – she looked empty, her face expressionless as the dead, looking intently at something nobody else could see, as if she were reliving those moments of horror constantly, not wanting to get rid of them, or to hide herself from the reality.

It was as if Saanjh was chastising herself for expecting too much from life, as if she was murdering that spirit inside her, that spirit which had shone so brightly only two days ago.

Her aunt was trying to talk to her, to console her, to love her and support her. She was doing everything she could to try and make Saanjh feel better. Her uncle, too, had been crying, though he had got Sooraj arrested, and had him bashed enough. But no amount of pain inflicted upon him could compensate for the pain that Saanjh had been going through, and his eyes bore a sense of acknowledgement of reality, as if he knew that everything was over for her. Even though he would ensure strict punishment, and many years of imprisonment for that beast, he knew that he could never set life back to normal for his daughter.

Veer didn't know by what force, or for what reason, but he found himself making his way through the crowd, towards Saanjh, kneeling before her at the edge of the *charpoi*, at a little distance from her the stumps of her legs as they hung, just slightly, over the edge. He positioned himself right in front of her, looking intently at her with a sadness that filled his eyes with tears.

It took Saanjh a while to recognise his face, but, when she did, she remained still for a moment, and then, tears started gushing from her eyes and, to everybody's surprise, she put her arms around him, rested her head on his shoulders and began to weep uncontrollably. "I have no strength left," she cried, sobbing and shaking him with her sobs. "Even death doesn't want me."

Veer could only wrap his arms around her and console her, listening patiently to her painful outbursts and comforting her with his hand, constantly patting her head. He could sense what Saanjh had in store for her, in the future because in Indian societics, all losses were acceptable to an extent, but not the loss of a woman's honour.

A woman's life came to a complete halt for no fault of hers, except that she possessed a vagina and hence was entitled to suffer all kinds of oppressions and exploitations. This loss of honour, which was a greater tragedy than the loss of her life was evident in each pair of eyes that stood watching the '*tamasha*' (racquet) that ensued in that courtyard, and secretly they also cursed that man who had saved her from drowning in the lake because death was more welcome than this honour less life.

Veer felt disgusted at this hypocritical society, which has been from the start of civilisation, relating rape to a woman's loss of honour rather than implicating the man, the one who actually perpetuates this loss to fulfil his 'need'.

177

"Everything will be all right, I'll make everything okay," he kept repeating, unaware of how or why, but continuing to hold Saanjh in a tight embrace, tapping her shoulders and head.

The entire town watched them with gaping eyes, even the uncle and aunt couldn't understand Saanjh's reaction. They looked at each other, an idea springing into their minds.

As Veer sat consoling Saanjh, not once did Mira cross his mind. Fate had played its game.

*

Veer was seething inside but he didn't know how to escape the predicament that had befallen him. Before he could even come to terms with reality, he was married to Saanjh. The Earth felt a fatal wound when his hand drew the vermillion powder, known as the 'sindoor', at the centre of Saanjh's head, in between the centre-parting of her hair.

All marriage rituals had been redundant thereafter – the red vermillion had lost its significance, in contrast to the high esteem it enjoyed in case of Mira.

Veer was frustrated and raging with helplessness in his heart for being unable to stop this impending doom. More than that, he was angry at Saanjh's uncle and aunt for being such opportunists. He had gone to console Saanjh and support her in a time of strife, but what had they done? They had misunderstood his care and concern. They had suggested an alternative to get them married, and everyone had been overjoyed, because someone was going to return the honour of this helpless girl by marrying her.

What about his Mira? What was to become of Veer and Mira? Mira was his wife, his true wife in all senses, whom he loved with all his soul. How was he going to face Mira?

There were people praising Veer for the strength of his character, almost the entire town revered him for being a Man in the true sense, and taking under his wing this shattered girl, by marrying her.

In his head swarmed a multitude of questions regarding right and wrong, fair and unfair and most importantly, questions about his future, and hers. Was getting married to him, the only way out of Saanjh's crisis? Couldn't he and the family support her, educate her further and set up a business with her, to make her independent? Couldn't she have thought of a better living, rather than agreeing to entrust herself into the hands of yet another man? Why was marriage the only solution to the problems in a woman's life?

Veer thought of Mira, how different and simple she was, never drooling over people for support. That was the kind of woman he admired. But then, in the first place, it had been Saanjh's strength and spirit that had caught his attention.

He thought of his father. How could his father agree to this marriage, swayed by sympathy and emotion, ready to sacrifice his son's life for a cause, under the pretext of saving somebody's honour? There was a basic flaw in the mindset, he concluded. Marriage could not be the only solution to problems like those of Saanjh and others like her.

How could Veer accept Saanjh as his wife when he knew that he belonged to Mira, every inch of him belonged to Mira, and even his soul belonged to Mira. But still he hadn't found the courage to refute the calamity that had occurred to him. He had been unable to stop the nuptial rites from taking place, at the cost of three lives. For the first time in his life he had inadvertently let Fate decide. Maybe, he thought, Mira would understand and move on, maybe Mira was not so important at all, or maybe he would be able to get over her, someday.

'No!' his mind interjected, and he shut his eyes as he sat in an empty room, following his wedding to Saanjh.

The '*sindoor*', '*mangalsutra*' and '*phere*', those nuptial rites that had been of such great importance to him earlier, now held meagre significance. Where, in the case of Mira, these rites had meanings and emotions attached, that day he had felt them to be mere fetters of society, a kind of bondage –a bondage which, in the name of courage and sympathy, had made him sin. Something which, in the pretext of saving one woman's honour, had led to the dishonour of another woman, his woman, the one who was waiting for him back home, unaware of the grievous infidelity he had committed.

Veer was ashamed of himself. Why had he not been able to take a stand for himself? He had never been so passive, especially when he knew that Mira's happiness was at stake, then what had made him take the '*pheras*'? What had made him be disloyal to Mira? What? His mind was a parade of such questions, but he had no answers. He kept repeating his plea of forgiveness, from God and from Mira.

180

He thought he should not return to her. He should not face her. He should vanish from her life, but he knew he couldn't. Mira had a right to know. Mira had a right to interrogate him for his decision. She had a right to hate him for doing this to her.

"Mira, Mira, Mira!" he exploded, his face red and eyes gushing with tears.

Veer was an ardent religious man and he prayed to God for strength and patience, for he was losing control of himself. Something that rarely happened to him, but then, not every day was his life so uncontrollably out of his hands. He needed Mira, and he needed her right away, to soothe his inner conflict just with her presence, to make him, believe, that he hadn't done anything wrong, that Fate was omnipotent and hence irrevocable. Yes, Fate was responsible for all the mess he was a part of. Fate.

In his heart, he knew that it wasn't enough to blame others or Fate. He was essentially in the wrong. He had chosen to be quiet on the issue of his marriage to Saanjh because, maybe, he didn't want to let go of the courageous persona that he had donned. He didn't want to remove himself from his new status, as the protector of a damsel in distress. He couldn't bring himself to step back from the responsibility that had been thrust upon him. However, he knew that he was not of this sort and, most importantly, Mira knew he wasn't like that. It was all a play of his mind to think of himself with such contempt. The reason was simple – Veer had been unable to say 'No' to Saanjh, when they had wanted to her marry him, their pleading eyes extorting out of him the consent. That's it. He couldn't say 'No' and nothing else mattered.

181

Veer wanted to leave the place very desperately. All the rituals stood meaningless to him. His anger subsided slowly because he had none but himself to blame. Indeed, the entire process of marriage and post marriage rituals were futile. Saanjh had hardly smiled through the entire procession. For him, smiling had been out of the question. Only her uncle and aunt had seemed relieved and happy, while his parents exhibited a feigned happiness. They knew their son had made a huge sacrifice.

'How hypocritical was the society,' he thought, that they turned a blind eye to all the trauma that Saanjh's rape and attempted suicide had wrought on each of their faces, and how that day they behaved as if everything was happening as naturally as it should. He wondered whether he was the only person who felt this way, or was everybody secretly affected by the same questions. Could they be so hollow inside, so as to not care about it, or were they so impertinent to feign happiness in the name of marriage.

Saanjh's uncle came forward and put her hand in his, swayed a number of hundred-hundred-rupee notes about their head and gave them to the servants. Veer removed his hand at once. Of course she felt it. He was abhorred by her touch, as he would be by any other woman's touch, except Mira's. It was a curse to him. He decided never to tell Saanjh about Mira, because letting go of the past was the only way out of a distorted present. Moreover, he was unsure of how Saanjh would take it. She might feel betrayed once again and he didn't want to shatter her hopes, whatever hopes she had from this relationship.

However, Veer could never give Saanjh the rights she

deserved as his lawfully wedded wife. He was being bound by the same shackles from which he was unravelling her, and also binding Mira in the process.

"I have to say something to you," he whispered to Saanjh, sitting just by his side.

She nodded signalling him to continue.

"I shall always be at your side, till the last of my breath. But... I shall never be able to give you the love that a wife expects out of her husband. We began as friends, let's fulfil this responsibility as friends," he spoke quietly, but looking intently at her.

Saanjh returned his gaze as a tear trickled down the corner of her empty eyes and she nodded again, this time with a sense of understanding.

That was the only conversation they had till the time they came back to Delhi and he told Mira everything. Three lives had been stalled – a beautiful friendship and a pious love story had been sacrificed because of this interplay of Fate.

183

CHAPTER TWENTY ONE

Mira sat on the floor of Veer's apartment. He sat next to her, narrating the story of his marriage to Saanjh. She sat at a considerable distance from him, making sure that no part of her was in contact with him, because he did not belong to her anymore. He was not her Veer anymore. He belonged to some other woman, and within a more sacrosanct relationship.

In spite of all that had passed between them, she had a peculiar sense of satisfaction, for he had done the right thing. He had saved a life by sacrificing his own. His goodness and humanity had ripped Mira of her dreams, love and him – the latter being an embodiment of the first two. She could feel him looking intently at her and she knew that a part of him was struggling to leave everything behind, to escape with her into a parallel world.

Veer's eyes were direct and cold as stone, for he knew somewhere in his heart that he had done the right thing.

Mira too, could sense the righteousness in his eyes and it was at that moment when she decided that she would not let him be right. He gave up on her, for humanity, but now she would show him what she was capable of – she would give up on him. Of course, Mira had no other choice. She couldn't wrong

184

Saanjh by continuing her relationship with him, so giving up on him was the only way out of this God gifted triangle.

She came back to her senses. Her eyes were on Veer, though she was not looking at him. Tears ran down her face, a hot stream of fresh salt water. Her nose was red and all the was kohl washed away. What was left behind was only emptiness, an emptiness that would remain with her for years to come. She staggered as she gathered herself, both literally and metaphorically. She had to collect up all the pieces of her soul that he had shattered, only this time there were more pieces for Mira to collect and put back together, more pieces than he held together all these years.

Veer cried bitterly, unafraid to express his emotions in front of her. Of course, it wasn't as if he didn't love her, something like that was beyond the scope of doubt. He could feel her breaking inside, shattering, one piece at a time, but he had no right to hold her together. He had lost all rights over her because he had wronged her and he was going to pay for this sin, all through his life.

What could have gone wrong in an essentially perfect relationship like theirs? Naturally, Fate had to intervene to draw them apart, not for a moment, but for the rest of their lives.

Mira did not say a word, because she was a confluence of emotions inside. She wanted to cry her heart out, howl, create an uproar out of her misery, but the searing pain in her heart benumbed her. She didn't understand what to say or how to react. There were a multitude of things that she wanted to speak of, but then words would dilute the trauma that had

185

gripped her inside out. She thought it best to leave, so she picked up her bag and slowly turned to walk out of the apartment.

He sat there on the floor, limp and lifeless, staring at her, but doing nothing because there was nothing left for him to do except to watch her leave. She was lost to him forever and he knew that very well. Tears streamed down his puffy red eyes, which harboured the same emptiness that Mira experienced.

She stopped for a moment at the door and turned around to face him. Veer slowly gathered himself up to his feet. The next moment the two souls were wrapped in a divine embrace of passion, love, tears and a multitude of other emotions they had no name for and couldn't express.

Mira held him tightly, pressing herself completely against his body and he responded with equal vigour, holding her tight and very close to him. It seemed Time was spinning in circles around them, trying to pull them apart, but that one moment they had been able to steal from Fate and, in that one moment, they strived to gather the most of each other into themselves. Their love of six years and commitment of a lifetime stood between them acting, not as a wall, but as a magnet which drew them closer together.

Ages had passed when they drew apart, though each of them hoped that one moment could convert to an entire lifetime. Their eyes searched each other's faces, digesting the features and outlines into their hearts forever. They also had a question – a question to their respective fates – Why were they brought to such a halt? Why couldn't they be together forever?

186

It was Mira, who spoke first, in a voice obstructed with tears and despair. "I love you," she said, barely a whisper, but enough to break his heart twenty times over.

Veer could not control his tears, burdened by the double weight of losing her and also wronging her. He managed to utter a choked, "I love you forever..." in return, the 'forever' barely escaping his lips.

Mira could not see him break down though it was evident that on the inside, his heart had turned to ashes. She knew he would hold himself responsible for everything and she had to show him that it was not his fault. In fact, he had done the right thing.

She held his face in her hands. "You have not done anything wrong, Veer," she said, words escaping between her heaving sobs and hot tears, "What you did was the right thing to do." She was surprised at herself for articulating those words. After a slight pause, she continued, "I will always be your first wife," she said, slowly and smiling through her tears, 'and never the other woman,' her heart added.

Veer foraged into her eyes, going deeper and searching for forgiveness, but all he could see was her soul drifting away from his own. He was reminded of that dazzling day when he had secretly sealed his relationship with Mira by taking the '*saat phere*' with her around a single lighted candle in his apartment. Hand in hand, they had walked in circles, around the candle and had voiced their vows, to be honoured and followed throughout their lives. They had never been the 'boyfriend-girlfriend' kind, giving way to a higher commitment and being the 'husband-wife' always. He could see himself in her eyes.

Mira understood what he was thinking about so she repeated her earlier statement. "I will always be your first wife."

Veer clasped her in his arms, pressed her close to his body and landed his lips on hers, crushing them with great passion and intensity, an infinite force in that infinite moment. He had wanted all of her in that one moment and he had wanted to give her all the love he had promised to her in that lifetime.

Mira too, had seized the moment and responded to his kiss with full dynamism. It was the last of what she would take of him and it was the last of what she would give him.

It was the last magic they had created together. Their kiss was salty, but it lasted a lifetime and not one of them cared to draw apart. Why would they? They had belonged to each other and now they were being drifted apart by Fate in a cruel turn of events. How much more welcome death would have been, they thought, rather than this unwanted and indefinite separation that would lodge them into despair for the rest of their lives.

With great strength Mira disconnected herself from his embrace and ran out of the room without a last look. She could not be in the wrong – she wasn't kissing her Veer, but Saanjh's lawfully wedded husband. The truth was that Veer belonged to her no more.

Mira was hardly in her senses to be able to realise anything. She had walked out of his apartment, knowing that he had broken down on the floor watching her leave, but she could not go back to him. The constant stream of tears had blurred her sight and made her dizzy. She had taken the elevator instead of the stairs. There was a sense of urgency in her actions as she had pressed the elevator button and waited for the door to open, frantically wiping away the tears from escaping her eyes and holding herself from collapsing. She was desperate to get out of his apartment, his world, and his life as soon as she could.

The beep of the elevator had come as a relief and she stood impatiently for its door to open, but when it finally did, she saw a woman in a wheelchair inside the elevator, a woman who had a very pretty face, but was disabled – Saanjh, Veer's wife. Behind her stood his mother, holding the wheelchair.

Mira stood trembling at this tumultuous throw of Fate. Naturally, her tears could no longer be held back, they had been unstoppable for the past one hour and a half.

Saanjh and Veer's mother stepped out of the elevator as they stood in front of Mira. His mother had tears in her eyes and Mira had sensed that she understood her pain. She gathered herself and bent down to touch the elder lady's feet to seek her blessing, as a token of respect. His mother stopped her midway and hugged her, as warmly as a mother would do. They had not exchanged words, but enough was said between them.

Disengaging from Veer's mother, Mira had then turned to face Saanjh. The latter's eyes spoke of the horrors she had been through.

Saanjh, however, had not known about this woman called Mira, for her eyes showed no glimpse of recognition. They were barren and desultory.

189

Looking at Saanjh sitting before her, Mira had been sure that indeed, Veer had done the right thing and that it was mere Fate that had tricked the three of them. She smiled at her and had bent forward to plant a sweet, tear soiled kiss on Saanjh's cheek, leaving abruptly for the elevator. As the door had closed, Mira saw Saanjh and Veer's mother with eyes full of tears, smiling at her. She could not smile back at them.

CHAPTER TWENTY TWO

Mira had been very quiet for the next two days at her house. She had missed college, locked herself up in her room for most of the time, and had been trying very hard to hide her tears from her family members, especially her mother. Clearly, the act of hiding had been futile because she soon realised the need to break the news to her family, as the day of their intended meeting with Veer was fast approaching.

The only thing that had withheld her from explaining her plight, had been the lingering uncertainty of the future. One thing had been certain – Mira could not tie herself in matrimony to another man. She couldn't bring herself to that pass, couldn't accept such infliction of pain.

However, it had been her father, that Mira was worried about. It was certain that he would never understand what her love had meant, what it had entailed, what it had forsook and what it had demanded out of her being. He would never understand the kind of love that his daughter had for a man whom he had not known at all. A man who had betrayed his daughter for another woman. No father could allow his daughter to pine away her life in solitude for the love of a man who was a betrayer.

191

She had to think of a way to work that out.

She even contemplated suicide. She had all the reasons in the world to want to end her life, but Mira had been a survivor. One couldn't exactly call her as a fighter, but she was definitely a survivor. She couldn't kill herself because that would push Veer into guilt forever. She would have escaped the pain and suffering of being separated from him, but his life would have ended up in darkness and guilt, pushing him deep into oblivion. Mira had never wanted to punish Veer. She had just wanted him back. Desperately. Something, that had been beyond the scope of the universe. There could be no chance of them getting back together, especially as long as Saanjh had lived.

The two days that Mira had spent crying incessantly, for the entire night, refusing to eat, and malfunctioning to the extent that it had been alarming to her family members. She had her phone switched off, lest Veer called and made her lose control over herself. She had decided to leave the city, and move somewhere away from him.

She sat on her bed, alone, staring hard at the wall. She had wanted reality to cease to exist and wake her up from the nightmare. Her eyes were puffy and red, her face pale and hair dishevelled but it had been her demeanour, which was alarming – listless and dead. Mira had made up her mind. It was high time she took the reigns of her life in her hands. With a misty stratagem in her head, she had decided to confide in her mother.

*

The same evening they were together for tea. Mira's

mother had been extremely worried for her, but she had been allowing Mira time to pull herself together, on her own. However, she had not failed to notice her daughter's red and swollen eyes, that had no life in them. She had not failed to notice wet patches on Mira's pillow early morning, because she had been crying all night, and neither had she failed to notice dark streams of evaporated tears on her face as she slept in the morning, looking pale and disease afflicted.

Mira sat looking down at the tea, stirring it with a spoon all the time. With each revolution that the spoon made in the tea cup, she had been gathering strength to face the reality. She had looked up at her mother only to find her looking patiently at her. Her eyes bore warm concern, but also a big question.

Mira had finally managed to speak,"I have resigned from college," she stated looking straight at her mother, observing her reactions and preparing herself to speak further. "I have planned to move out of Delhi," she continued, looking intently at her mother and expecting questions in return.

Her mother delved deep into her eyes, probing further and further for an answer, for a reason behind her daughter's queer behaviour, but all she could see was sorrow, despair and an eerie emptiness as if her body had been ripped off her soul. She moved forward to embrace her daughter and in a moment, Mira lay broken and sobbing in her mother's arms. Her breathing was heavy and she had been unable to speak further. Her mother feared the worst of things, pertaining to the safety of women in their city. Not once had she thought that something could have been wrong between her daughter and Veer. She had known him well enough

193

to know that he could never do anything to hurt Mira. She had witnessed the ardour of his love while at the hospital.

She sat comforting her daughter, wiping away the hot tears streaming down her young face, as she spoke to her in one of her most affectionate ways, "Mira, listen to me, look up, look up, Mira and tell me what happened?" she asked her politely.

Mira lifted her gaze to face her mother, pain and heartbreak overflowed through her eyes, and she gathered some strength, "*Maa*, it's Veer," a barely audible whisper escaped her lips, "I lost him," she had continued, her head hung terribly low and blinded by her own tears.

Her mother had known what Veer had meant for her daughter. She too, had experienced the pain of unrequited love when Mira's father had been unable to reciprocate her love. She held her daughter in a tight embrace, resting her head sideways on her shoulder and pulling back strands of Mira's hair to clear her face, "tell me what happened?" she said softly.

Gradually Mira began to speak, initially in between heavy sobs, but then composing herself. She didn't want her mother to think of Veer as a betrayer. He was not a betrayer. Though it had been a meddling of Fate to pull them apart from each other, it didn't alter the fact that he had betrayed her, even though he had been compelled under other obligations.

Mira's mother had heard her story as tears kept fluxing in and out of her eyes. She comforted her daughter and wiped away her tears. She wished to take away all her pain, but such wishing could never be fulfilled because her daughter would have to bear the pain of separation on her own.

"*Maa*, please don't think he's wrong, *Maa* please, I know... I know Veer got caught up in circumstances, you know he is not of that kind."

Mira kept entreating her mother, but the elder woman understood the sacrifice which that man had made. She did not blame him for anything but she had to hold her daughter together.

"Mira, I know, I completely understand that Veer must not be blamed. He married a disabled woman, you must understand how brave he is, how least self serving. Just remember him as a beautiful past, learn from it and let go of him," her mother completed, hoping to make her daughter understand that running away from home and family could not be a solution to the problem. Mira had to understand that not all relationships were meant to be fulfilled. One had to learn to let go of the past – beautiful or painful.

"Mira," she continued, "running away is no solution. You don't have to leave Delhi or go to any other place. Stay here and I promise we will help you get over Veer. Please my dove, you don't have to go anywhere," she had entreated.

However, Mira was an adamant soul, "No *Maa*!" she blurted, looking straight into her eyes, "I don't want to let go of Veer!" She paused for her feelings to get registered in her mother's mind, "never," came the final affirmation, "*Maa*, I want to live with him for the rest of my life, I want to keep all his memories and live with them till the time I can," she completed.

Her mother had known that Mira meant every word she said. She could make out how deeply involved she was in this act and had nothing here to stop her – a forced marriage to a stranger, perhaps. No, she couldn't allow that for her daughter and she decided to stand with Mira in her decision. She had held Mira's hands while her daughter kept pleading, "*Maa* I have lived my life in the past six years, please let me have them forever."

Her mother nodded softly, "Mira," she had paused to avoid her own grief, "I will not stop you my child," tears gushed down her own eyes, partly at her daughter's grief and partly because of her own, pertaining to the separation from her. Her daughter had grown up and she had to let her go.

*

For Mira, the future lay misty and her plans had been incomplete, but they had to be executed as soon as possible. With each breath, she inhaled memories of her past life. She had decided to leave Delhi forever and move to Sikkim. It was a place of her choice because she had fallen in love with the serenity and beauty of that corner of India when once she had been there on a family vacation. Moreover, it was remote and less likely to make her face people, especially friends and relatives. The only thing that was certain was the fact that she had to leave.

However, before the Sikkim hurdle there was yet another hurdle before Mira. Her father. She had known that expecting him to understand such a decision by his young unmarried daughter was similar to asking God for a miracle to set things right. She had decided to leave without telling him as

196

that might prevent unnecessary hassles. Though she had been worried about how he would react to the fact that his daughter had taken a big decision on her own, and most importantly, without his approval. Mira was also worried that her mother and siblings would have had to bear the grunt of his anger and she was deeply worried about them.

She could not forego her decision. There had been an abundance of pain inside her and she had to let it all out, to get herself healed and repaired. Otherwise, she would not be able to refrain from getting suicidal.

The day when Mira had to leave, she decided to inform her father about it through a letter. She had believed that it would result in the purgation of all her emotions and feelings. It hadn't been easy for her to write one, since she had never been so upfront and personal with her father before. However, life had evolved differently and she had to act according to its demands. Her father had to understand. He had no choice.

Dear Papa,

With due respect, I am attempting to draft out this letter to explain my predicament to you. I have a vague idea of what your reaction will be after reading it, but there are things about this daughter of yours that you must know, because I want you to know.

To be honest, there were many times in the past twenty-six years of my life when I wanted you to understand me, but with time I concluded that there existed a fundamental difference in the way we thought. I'm sure you feel the same difference too. You know, today, as I sit down to tell you things about my past, present and future, I have this flicker of hope that you will understand what I mean to say. Maybe, you can try, for my sake.

Papa, I remember spending good times with you. I remember being happy to see you. I remember feeling attached to you, but I don't understand how all that changed over time. I don't understand, or I don't remember, how all my feelings changed to the complete opposite. All this time, I felt I hated you so much and then I would feel all concerned for you. This duality has restrained me from expressing my true intentions to you, both positive and otherwise. When I think of the reason that I drifted away from you, it is only your drunken brawls that come to my mind, and I have to shut my eyes tight to evade those images, because I do not want to re-live them, nor do I want to remember you like that. But, do you remember it?

You know, the last time you hugged me was after I survived that fortunate accident two years back. On that day I once again experienced the same feelings towards you, as if I was still a three year old, basking in your love from morning to night. But did you notice what took you away from me, and from the rest of us? Did you realise that you were hurting your family, under the influence of something totally unrelated to us? It was your relationship with alcohol. You don't realise Papa, how it has corroded you, how it has schemed against you, blocking all health and happiness from touching you.

Papa, I may not be the perfect student, you wanted me, or all of us, to be. I may not have cleared entrance examinations and scored 95% and above in twelfth standard. I may not have chosen to study what you wanted me to study, but I have always strived to be a good daughter for you and, so have all of us, strived to have perfect relationships with you. Be it Maa, Anu or Aditya – all of us have strived to be your perfect family, but do you realise where the lag occurred? Do you realise how we never expected you to be the perfect father, but just a father to us instead of only the head of the family, that you're always intent on being.

Today, I am going to be upfront and honest with you, because this may be my last chance to tell you all that is buried in my heart. Do you know why I cherish the accident that took place two years ago? Why I call it fortunate? I call it so, because I thought it had given my sober father, the old loving and cheerful father back to me. I thought I could have a hundred accidents for that one moment of your fatherly affection and the togetherness of our family, and a lot has changed since, between you and us, and especially between you and mother, that I feel blessed to have had a chance to lie on my deathbed and watch my family draw closer.

I guess I have already digressed enough, don't want to make this letter painfully long for you. Anyway, how can a person spill out twenty-six years of unspoken words in a letter of a mere thousand? Let me, anyhow, come to the purpose of this letter and, you know, frankly, I'm not very good at speaking my thoughts, though I believe I am comprehensible in writing. So, that is why this white sheet and this pen came to my rescue when I wished to talk about the most crucial decision of my life to the most important person concerned.

Remember Veer, the person I wanted to marry? And I said that we were bound to be together, no matter what?

My, my I was strong and certain back then, when I

had that person's support, but today I stand alone with all my strength drained away, because I have no clue how to tell you that your twenty-six year old, unmarried daughter has decided to give up on this world, on the life you envisioned for her. No, I have no intention of ending my life, or anything of that kind. I just have this ardent wish to start afresh. I know it doesn't sound conventional. In fact, it sounds stupid, especially for an aging father of a young daughter, but please, this time your daughter has left you with no option but to comply with her demands. Throughout life, Maa kept telling me that I was a lot like you, that my stubbornness was a gift from your genes, but I never believed her, except today, when I realise how correct she was, because I feel that urge inside me to listen to nobody but my heart.

I do not wish to spill out my plans to you before I'm ready with them, because I know you will come and take me back home, something I don't want. Just know that I'll be safe and secure, wherever I'll be, and I will always be my parents' daughter. Other relationships have no meaning for me and I don't wish to build any more in the future. Life, for me has been what it had to be, and I don't wish to give it another chance.

Papa, please don't worry. I am way beyond mature enough to take care of myself, and now, you have to be mature enough to release your hold on your daughter's life. Please let me have a chance to build my life according to my, reasonable, wishes and trust me, so that I know I have the support of my family. I may not be your perfect child, but I wish to be the perfect human being in my own eyes. I promise to take care of myself and I promise that you shall be proud of me, someday!

I have to leave now. I don't have much time. I promise I will write again, once I'm settled in mind and place. Please take care of yourself and the others, especially Maa – I'm leaving behind a part of my soul there in Delhi, in all your hearts, please keep it safe and happy.

Time to go, I guess. Endless tears can't rid me of this pain, that is so overbearing I wish to drown in it, but my family shall be the key to keeping me afloat and that key is a united structure of you, Maa, Anu and Aditya. Be safe and take care.

Yours lovingly,
Mira

P.S. Never really got a chance to say it to you and the others in person, so let me write it down for you, especially, I LOVE YOU.

After numerous attempts at writing this letter, Mira had finally drawn one out and, after reading and re-reading it, at least seventeen times, she had left it at her father's bedside. After which, she left straight for the airport. She had not allowed any of her family members to come see her off, because tearing apart from them seemed an impossible task, to her. Her mother had already been crying incessantly. Embracing them all in a final touch, she sat in the cab and left. Her tears wouldn't stop, but Mira had to disconnect, and so, she did. She disconnected completely from her twenty-six year old life.

And began a new one.

SIKKIM

CHAPTER TWENTY THREE

Mira came back to the present, as softly as she had drifted into the past and, in her eyes there dawned a flicker of recognition, hiding the latent emotions of a leftover past.

Her mind acknowledged the present setting as she came to terms with what she saw in front of her. The sun now hid behind the dark clouds that had developed over the lake, at the same height as where she sat, and enveloped her in a dark mist. The weather had turned, and there stood a strong possibility of rain. The slight breeze had not stopped, it was slowly carrying away the lighter clouds, but heavier ones hung over the lake, creating a shadow and blocking the setting rays of the sun.

She closed her eyes and tears ran down her cheeks onto the palms of her hands. There was a slight pain in her eyes and she felt feverish. That is what generally happened when she had been crying for a long time – the constant influx of tears and their subsequent evaporation left her eyes itchy and irritable.

Her mind was blank now, and she saw nothing when her eyes were shut, maybe blackness and motley of lights, but nothing absolute. Her face was expressionless, and she could hear the sounds of the

203

rumbling clouds, but nothing else. She was still twirling the dried oak leaf between her fingers, some of it had crumbled, and fallen on her dress, but she wasn't concerned about that. Her mind welcomed the first thought after several moments of emptiness, 'Senescence is the only certainty,' she pondered, a new thought taking shape in her mind. If death was the only certainty, then why was she wasting away her life waiting for another human being? The world was a big place and, surely, there must be some place for her in it, so then, why did she suffer, suspended in this limbo.

A new kind of smile spread across her face. "Let me show Veer that I can do better without him," she whispered to herself. "Yes, let me write more and earn a name for myself," she continued, "and then, maybe, I could start an organization of my own, a place for the abandoned elderly and people with disabilities. A place to give people independence. And choices." She smiled, feeling a sudden spark light up inside her. "I am going to carve out a niche for myself," she asserted, almost with the enthusiasm of a child, who wishes to have a new profession every week.

Mira realised that this future was exactly what she wanted. She didn't need a man to stabilize her life. She, alone, was enough for that. She looked down upon her hand, the one with the oak leaf, which was coiled in a fist, crushing the leaf in her palm. She opened the fist, brought it to the level of her chin and, then, with one breath, she blew away the pieces of the oak leaf and, with it, the shattered pieces of her past washed into the vast abyss in front of her.

"Enough tears," she reprimanded herself, "get a life Mira! Get a reason to live. You have to love yourself, more than anyone else in the world," she squealed, still convincing herself on the last part of the sentence.

She had already begun framing a plot for her next novel, and it was going to be about the struggle of a young woman. A woman who would never give up. It would be about the extraordinary intellectual strength of that woman, and her will to survive. The thought of writing made her feel better, much more in control of herself, but, again, the clouds rumbled and she looked up at the sky. She hadn't realised it had become so dark. There was lightning in the distance and, suddenly, a raindrop landed on her trousers, instantly seeping through to touch her skin.

"Rain at this time of the year?" she wondered, "maybe the universe is debating over my condition," she mocked herself as she lifted her head to look up at the sky once more. Another drop of rain landed on her forehead. 'Oh no, no, no! I must reach home. I must not get drenched in the rain,' she thought as she stood up, gathering herself and all her belongings in one hand. As she stood up, she looked around at the valley once again, "This is it," she said loud and clear, "Next time, I won't come here for help, I'll come here to share my victory with you!"

She spoke to Nature, and her words floated along with the clouds. There were tears in her eyes as she spoke. Another drop of rain hit her and the wind gathered speed. "All right, I'm leaving," she laughed, "you don't have to push me away." Then, she left the place, walking barefoot to her house.

Only Fate was there to observe, and mock this dalliance of Mira and Nature, as the two forces communicated with each other, almost as friends.

The homeward journey was uphill and it would take her twenty to thirty minutes to get there. "What made me wear stilettos today?" she grumbled to herself, looking at the desolate pair in her hands, as they glittered.

The weather was worsening. The winds were gaining momentum and the clouds were getting duskier, and they seemed bloated as if waiting for a signal to pour out onto the Earth below. They reminded her of a pregnant woman just on the verge of delivery, just as the clouds stood on the verge of delivering.

A dim thought seeped into her mind darkening her expression, "I will never have a child of mine own," she whispered to herself softly, allowing the grief of that thought to sink into her psyche. 'No more of yearnings Mira, be happy with what you have,' her mind interjected, checking the dejection from invading her system once again.

She shook her head to ward off unnecessary thoughts away and pulled the overcoat closer to her body, the wind was not only getting fierce but also cold. She entered a region, on the way home, where there were long, shooting trees on either side of the road and, at that moment, they were swaying dangerously because of the wind. There had been many instances of trees falling onto pedestrians and vehicles, crushing them to the ground.

Mira quickened her steps. She was afraid and almost running, now. She was all alone, there was no one else to be seen in the vicinity. Naturally, who would have dared to venture out in the storm?

It took her five minutes of brisk walking to reach the lowest step of the hill on which her haven was situated. Gradually, her breathing relaxed but with each step she climbed, her heart was palpitating furiously. "Oh, this storm has caught my nerves," she said to herself, but silently she was grateful that it hadn't started raining properly yet.

When she reached her garden, she saw that the silver oaks were dancing furiously to the rhythm of the wind, the top of the trees whirling in circles. The effect was pretty and Mira smiled as she observed them.

She turned to move towards the door and slid one hand into her coat pocket to reach for the key, but she found something else inside. It was a dried oak leaf, completely intact. There was a momentary pause, in her eyes, and in her movements, as she stood staring at the leaf, but she avoided any other thoughts, concentrating only on using that leaf as a bookmark.

As she reached the door, she realised that it was not locked, and she opened it, wondering what had kept Koicha from her usual reading at this time of the day, causing her to leave the door unlocked.

Mira stepped inside and left the stilettos near the steps. She looked around for her housekeeper and, as she turned left into the hall, she froze.

CHAPTER TWENTY FOUR

Eleven years had passed, and, still she stood where she had left him. The places had changed. The surroundings had changed. The people had changed. Age had changed her as well, but her eyes remained the same, hidden beneath the lightly smudged kohl. Only it seemed, that they had lost their light. That spark had been dimmed the day she left him behind.

Not much had changed in him, though. He stood in the hall wearing dark blue jeans and a crimson shirt, topped with a black jacket. Despite the numerous times she had taught him that collar upon collar was a fashion faux pas, he had made the same mistake that day. She wondered if he had done it deliberately, or perhaps, it was her imagination. But there he was, after eleven years, standing in the square hall of her house, with his knees brushing against the adjacent sofa, the same height, build, face and smile, exactly as she remembered him.

Only his eyes seemed different to her, they weren't their sparkling usual. Maybe, it was the mist of her own eyes that she couldn't see deep or clearly enough. For a moment, her heart stopped pumping blood, rather it was pumping at such a furious speed that it benumbed her. After all, she had finally seen that face again after eleven years of pain and separation, eleven years of longing and yearning for his love, and his touch. She wanted to run to him, to embrace him with her full strength, to amalgamate him into herself. But that had all been lost eleven years ago and this thought brought her back to reality.

His presence was paralysing, overwhelming and she was about to black out as she staggered on one foot, attempting to hold on to the adjacent sofa, when he came to the rescue. "Mira," he said in a heavily choked voice and that was force enough to grip her, and to bring her back to her senses. Her name emanating from his lips had a healing effect on her, but she chose to remain silent.

At that moment Koicha came bustling out of the kitchen.

"*Saheb*, why are you standing?" she questioned him with a puzzled look.

Her eyes moved over to Mira, following the direction of his gaze and the moment she looked at her, a twinge of a smile appeared upon her lips. Her face reflected tranquillity and achievement.

Mira could see an idea of reconciliation in Koicha's misty eyes because, after all, she had been the one person who knew all about him and the only person who had been hopeful of his return to her. It was Koicha's turn to break the stupor that Mira had been sinking into.

"*Didi*, I knew you would be surprised. I was amazed to see *Saheb* at the door," she moved about the hall as they both stood rooted to their spots. Koicha continued, setting a tray of sandwiches and juices on the table in front of him. "I was so happy to see him," she rattled on, "ten years I have been working for you, staying with you and, today, I finally get to meet this man who, to me, seemed to reside only in the photographs on these walls," 'and in your eyes', she wanted to add, looking at Mira."Why are you both standing?" Koicha asked, and it was then that he took a seat and Mira sat down opposite him.

Gradually, Mira took control of the sudden burst of emotions inside her, and her lips broke into a quivering smile. A part of her yearned to touch him, and feel his presence for real. Her lips longed for that old, not faded, feeling of his lips upon hers, the beautiful sensation of emotions rushing from within both of them, and the struggle of their lips to overpower each other. Today, however, was different because one part of her wanted him to crush her under the burden of his love, but another part wanted freedom from his love. This surge of passion shaded with doubt, created a spark in her eyes and a sudden uneasiness around the centre of her breasts. Her gaze was broken by Koicha's interruption.

"*Didi*, see I got all the sweet dishes for *Saheb*, I know how much he loves them," she winked.

"I'll cook tonight," was all Mira could say. "Veer will have dinner with us."

Koicha left them alone in the hall, muttering to herself, excited that her dear *Didi* had finally had a chance to reunite with her *Saheb*. Little did she know, that this might not turn out to be a reunion, but an affirmation of the breaking of all bonds between them.

"How come you're in Sikkim?" Mira asked.

Veer made no reply, but simply kept looking at her. The emanation of his name from her lips, the assertion about him staying for dinner, had had an impact on him. He felt wanted from her. He felt possessed by her, still. He could not stop himself from looking at her.

Images kept reverberating in his head, images eleven years old, images of their togetherness and he too found it hard to fight through them and stay with reality. He thought of how he had come to Sikkim, only to see her, to find out whether she was all right, though there was never a moment in the past eleven years, when she hadn't lived in him. Yet her name in the newspaper had made his coming to her inevitable.

The journey to Sikkim, the search for Mira, and the happiness of finding her, had been all too much for him and now, as she sat before him, wearing a pastel pink high-necked sweater and a black coat with blue trousers, he couldn't take his eyes off her, no matter how much he had always hated high-necked clothes on her. He noticed her waist-length hair and he smiled inwardly. Mira had aged, and she had aged beautifully. He felt the need to hold her in his arms and kiss her nose, which was the only thing that hadn't changed. He wished to hold her tight and press her close to himself like he used to, eleven years ago.

Veer thought of her book, which he had read and re-read, and which had led him to her, to that house, and that hall, where he sat looking at a picture of them from their younger days, hanging on the opposite wall. The picture, he clearly remembered, was taken on their sixth anniversary, the last one they had had together. Tears welled up in his eyes and he struggled to hold them back. He saw copies of her recently published book, lying on the side table, and then he looked at her. He could not help himself from blurting out, "Beautiful".

Mira looked up at him all of a sudden, a mix of tears, blush and light in her eyes as she pierced him with her knowing, yet questioning, look.

"Beautiful," he repeated, looking straight into her eyes, "your book is beautiful."

She relaxed a bit, smiling through her tears, ineffective at hiding both. "When did you start reading books?"

'The day we parted,' was what Veer wanted to say, but he could not. "A long time ago," he told her. He had known all along, he had known that she would write, someday. He knew what a terrific writer, she was and he had been waiting for her book, only to reach out to her, and that was exactly what had happened.

"*Maa-Papa, Bhaiya-Bhabhi*, how is everyone?" she asked.

He knew that 'everyone' also comprised of people she didn't want acknowledge. He didn't want her to talk about 'everyone' at that moment. "Fine," he replied curtly.

Mira was not satisfied. She had to degrade herself further and she mustered courage to ask him, "How is," she paused, "how is your wife?"

Veer stopped. All the relishing and delving into the

past came, abruptly, to a halt. "She's fine," he said, tears welling up in his eyes, which were impossible to hide from her.

Mira looked at him with a strange sadness, wanting to embrace him, but stopping herself at the same time. She asked no further questions and allowed him time to get over that blow.

This had always been their story, even eleven years ago. She had a proclivity of bombarding him with questions, be it on a call, text, or in person, and he patiently replied to all her questions, never breaking the stream. Her questions had been never ending, as had been his replies but, now, of course, things were different.

They sat together for a while, each trying to read what the other was trying to say, each with an extended hand, trying to reach out to the other, but drawing back even at the slightest contact. "I don't think I will be able to stay for dinner tonight," he said, trying to figure out a way to build the burnt bridges between them.

"You won't be late. Manjhi *Bhaiya* will drop you to the hotel," she said, her tone confident yet pleading. She could not bring herself to ask where he was staying, here in Sikkim. She didn't want to know.

Veer could not say anything. He could see that Mira wanted to know more and he knew why she kept drawing a wall between them. He knew because she hadn't changed one bit. Eleven years ago, she would retreat into her shell, whenever they had a conflict. He knew she wanted to talk. He even knew that she had no words so he decided to fill the space with his own. "So what do you do, here in Sikkim?" he asked,

213

not looking at her, but with his eyes lowered, looking at his shoes.

"I teach English literature at the University of Sikkim," she replied.

"Oh, and you travel all by yourself?" he asked, his face lighting as he remembered what a bad driver she was.

"Manjhi *Bhaiya* drives me around and, sometimes, I prefer to walk," she replied meekly, liking the little bit of interaction between them. After a pause, she looked up at him.

He smiled at her and instantly she knew what he was thinking.

"Don't worry. I can drive pretty decently now," she said, observing how he was struggling to hold back his smile. She had longed for that smile. She had longed to see that spark dancing in his eyes as she saw the past enfolding in them. How he used to tease her about her driving, and how she wanted to prove him wrong!

"I didn't say anything," he replied, laughing through his misty eyes.

"I can read your eyes..." but she stopped speaking midway. "Have something," she blurted and, without looking at him, she passed him the plate of his favourite sweets.

Veer extended his hand to pick one, and she saw that it looked the same as it had been, while holding her, eleven years ago. His nails never fully trimmed, and the impartial golden black hair on his fingers. How she had known every inch of him, but then suddenly her gaze rested on his wedding ring. She lifted her eyes to look at him.

He knew what she was thinking. He wanted to say something, but now, he had no words.

Koicha called out from the kitchen, "*Didi*!" she came out into the hall, "everything is done, and you may come and cook. I'll leave now," she continued looking intently at Mira, then addressing him,"okay *Saheb*, See you tomorrow. *Namaste*."

Mira experienced sudden uneasiness as she came to terms with being alone in the house, alone with Veer.

He too strained a bit.

Their eyes met for a brief moment, enslaving them both in their old passions for each other, in that old longing for each other. She got up and went into the kitchen.

"*Didi*, call me if you need any help. I'm just here in the quarters," said Koicha.

It was at that moment that Mira realised what this stupid woman was planning to do. She was leaving early. Koicha, that crazy woman who never left until literally told to do so, she was leaving at eight that evening. She looked up at Koicha, trying to read her eyes, trying to project her own inhibitions at her but she only smiled back in answer. A smile that Mira understood, perhaps even Veer did, but never acknowledged it.

Koicha walked out through the rear door, leaving them alone in that three bedroom wooden house with a raging fire in the room as well as in their souls, but Mira had to disconnect. She had vowed, eleven years ago that she would never be in the wrong, and that she would never let him down. She would never be the 'other woman'.

Veer could read everything in her eyes, but he had no answer.

FINIS

ABOUT THE AUTHOR

Rashi Shrivastava is a twenty four year old woman, who holds a Masters Degree in English Literature from the University of Delhi. Reared in a convent school, she is an avid reader and writer by default. Writing fiction is something that came naturally to her, and she hopes to make it big as a bestselling novelist one day. Waiting for the pen to coincide with her thoughts and animate them into a beautiful book, she has finally been able to achieve a part of her dream. She has published a short story – 'The Yellow Envelope' in a compilation by Authors' Ink India, 'Love a Sweet Poison 2', in October 2016.

Rashi is also a regular blogger and writes about numerous aspects of life ranging from Books, Love, Writing, Reading and Beliefs. Her blog address is as follows: *www.temptationofwords.wordpress.com*. Besides, she is a writer on Facebook and Instagram for her page – Temptation Of Words, where she likes to put down her thoughts on display for her readers.

She believes in the charm of the universe being the best judge in giving people exactly what they deserve. Setbacks and failures are a part of life, but the glint of one small achievement has the potential to surpass all their gloom.

She can be contacted at –
writetorashishrivastava@gmail.com

Web address – http://rashishrivastava.in